STORIES FROM THE INKSLINGERS

A WRITTEN REMAINS ANTHOLOGY

Gryphonwood Press

Gryphonwood Press
545 Rosewood Trail, Grayson, GA 30017-1261

Published by Gryphonwood Press
www.gryphonwoodpress.com

Library of Congress Control Number: 2007904050

Edited by JM Reinbold and Ramona DeFelice Long
Designed by David Wood and JM Reinbold
Cover art and design by Justynn Tyme
Illustrations for *Baffled by the Green Door, Dead Man's Treasure, At Sea, Christmas Surprise, Compost, Street Smarts and Transfusions* by Sherry Thompson
Illustrations for *Les Fleurs Dementos* by Justynn Tyme
Production coordinated by Lightning Source.

ISBN 13: 978-0-9795738-0-4
ISBN 10: 09795738-0-7
Printed in the United States of America
First printing: October, 2007

MEET THE AUTHORS

Mary Jo DiAngelo lives and writes in Wilmington, Delaware.

"Compost" was written especially for this anthology while Mary Jo was a member of the Written Remains.

KB Inglee has lived in Delaware for thirty years. She interprets history at Greenbank Mill and Philips Farm, a living history museum, where she fosters the heritage live stock. Her book *Farmer's Daughter, Miller's Son* presents the life of the Philips family who lived at the farm in the early 1800s. She is past president of the Delaware Valley chapter of Sisters in Crime.

"In 'Dead Man's Treasure,' one man's treasure is another man's junk. Fortunately, Lottie and Virginia know the difference."

Jacquie Juers lives and writes in Wilmington, Delaware. Two of Jacquie's stories, "Questioning My Mother" (2002) and "Stand Up" (2005) were published in the literary magazine Thema. Her story "Reality Check" was the second runner-up in Out & About magazine's 9th annual short story contest. Jacquie is the current Treasurer for the Delaware Valley chapter of Sisters in Crime, and is a manager at Borders Books.

Ramona Long writes primarily for children and young adults. She currently lives in Delaware. She has received artist's fellowships through the Pennsylvania State Arts Council and the Delaware Division of the Arts.

"One of my uncles was killed in the Pacific during World War II and was buried at sea. In a Catholic family, where visiting relatives in the graveyard is an important and meaningful ritual, this is like a double loss. When writing 'At Sea', I wanted to explore the idea of sea burial as comforting, so that this uncle, who died long before my birth, would enjoy some fictional closure and, hopefully, peace."

MEET THE AUTHORS

JM Reinbold is the author of "Cernnunos: Ancient Celtic God." This essay was originally published by the Order of Bards, Ovates and Druids and has been reprinted dozens of times. It was included in Mything Links, an annotated and illustrated collection of links to mythologies, fairy tales, folklore, sacred arts and traditions. "Cernnunos…" has been translated into four languages.

Her short story, "The Mark of Cain" was purchased by the British role-playing game magazine *Valkyrie* in 1996. She is also the author of "Journey to Xibalba," which had its debut reading at the Wilmington Institute Library in October of 1995 as part of the Friday Night Art Loop series.

Other works, most notably "An Angel Unused to Air" and an excerpt from "West," a novella length story, appeared in *Bridges*, a literary magazine published by the Writers Workshop at Neumann College in 1996.

After years of trying to learn how to write a novel, something finally "clicked" and she is now close to completing her first book length manuscript. JM Reinbold lives in Wilmington, Delaware with her husband, son and seven rescued cats. She now writes every day, which took her an exceedingly long time to figure out was the "big secret" to writing and the one single thing that gets the words on the page and the work done!

"Transfusions," originally written in 1996, and rewritten in 2007 for this anthology, was the result of an unlikely confluence of ideas and events – late night discussions on the nature and ecology of God, a news report on the discovery of a previously unknown strain of the AIDS virus, a reading of Flannery O'Connor's novella *Wise Blood*, and a particularly thought provoking episode of the X-Files, plus a "secret ingredient" - and my first foray into the realms of Gothic or grotesque fiction and magical realism."

MEET THE AUTHORS

Greg Smith is the author of two suspense novels, a children's book and a collection of short stories. Prior to writing fiction full time, he spent more than a decade in public relations including PR director of a Washington, D.C. based public policy group. Recently, he led a grassroots campaign on behalf of major sports leagues including the NFL, NBA, Major League Baseball and the NCAA.

He has a BA in English from Skidmore College and an MBA from the College of William and Mary. His business writings and letters have appeared in The Washington Post, Washington Times, Expansion Management and Area Development.

He lives in Wilmington, Delaware with his wife and son.

Sherry Thompson lives in Wilmington, Delaware. Now that she's retired from the University of Delaware, where she worked for thirty-five years, she has been able to devote most of her time to writing. Twenty-five years ago she wrote the first draft of *Seabird* with lots of inspiration and no clue how to write. A much-revised *Seabird* received 3rd prize in the Genesis Award, SF/fantasy category in 2006, and will be published by Gryphonwood Press this autumn. (Extract available at: http://khivasmommy.googlepages.com/home) After completing final revisions of the novel, she intends to continue her work on its sequel, *Earthbow*, and eventually add other stories sharing the same fantasy world. She has also written a score of short stories. One of those stories, "Winter's Season," was published in the 2003 SF/F anthology edited by David Bain.

" 'Baffled by the Green Door' is largely autobiographical. I wrote it as a way of dealing with a number of sad incidents and mysteries from my childhood. Virtually every scene, person, and location in the story is as accurate as memory allows. However, I have combined events from several days into a few hours for 'dramatic purposes.' "

MEET THE AUTHORS

Justynn Tyme (a.k.a The Mage of Lunacy), like a blacksmith, forges his unique brand of artistic-ness by applying unique perspectives that derive from many internal elements in his personalities – base elements which are not normally found together in nature. Using his Buddhist comprehension, dada nature, and his absurdist outlook, coupled with his abnormal social idiosyncrasies, and strong creative drive, makes for a strange but amusing style of robust insanity, which is tempered into bite-sized works that explode, even in the most rigid of imaginations.

Justynn is currently ten feet tall and made entirely out of pickle - flavored pudding. He is the founder of the Whimsical Icebox, an absurdist comedy group, and creator and curator of the Dada Yow community. His work has appeared all around the internet in the most unlikely places. The likely places are in the pages of: The Whimsical Icebox, The Cult of Cod, Dada Yow, 391, The New Absurdist, 691, The Written Remains, The Dodsley Pages and Bust Down the Door and Eat All The Chickens. He spends many a lonely evening basting in a pot of boiling farina with his two cats and a plastic parrot. You can see and read more of Justynn's work at http://www.justynntyme.com or http://www.omphalosdada.org

" 'Les Fleurs Dementos' takes a fictitious approach to absurdism. So it must first be understood that there is, of course, a core philosophy to absurdism but there are also personal ideologies of what absurdism is or should be, much like the parts of a tree. They have their individual classification such as trunk, branches, roots and leaves. Yet individually these are not a tree. With that said all personal philosophies on absurdism are not absurdism without the core understanding as reference. At first glance absurdism can seem like "madness." And, in a sense, it is but this is not random insanity. Absurdism is the highlighting of the insanity born of perception. It is the futility of man's justification of life itself and of himself, which can not be controlled, defined or justified no matter how supreme humankind appears to be. It is the mentality between rationality and madness. It is the understanding that irrationality is the fundamental principle of human existence. Much like a man suddenly trapped in his own bathroom with only a head of lettuce."

Dedication

This book is dedicated to all members — past, present and future — of the Written Remains Writers Group.

Acknowledgements

The editors wish to thank everyone who contributed to the creation of the Inkslingers Anthology, with special thanks to David Wood and Gryphonwood Press.

The Written Remains Writers Group
P. O. Box 5906
Wilmington, DE 19808-0906

www.writtenremains.org

Introduction

The Written Remains Writers Group was founded in 1995, the year prior to my graduation from Neumann College. I didn't want to lose touch with the writers that I knew and worked with at Neumann, so some of us gathered together once a month to share our writing projects with one another. We circulated our stories and listened to the reactions of fellow writers in order to improve our work. Over the years, writers have come and gone. Of those four or five original members, only I am left; but the writers' group remains and continues to grow, enriched by new members and new stories.

People always want to know why our writers' group is called The Written Remains. Written Remains has a double meaning: First is that the written word is never lost. It remains preserved, physically and electronically, for future generations. The second refers to the end result of the writer's vision after it has been extracted from the imagination and committed to the page. No matter how beautifully, how clearly, how accurately we write, the resulting words are never quite as magnificent as the vision in the writer's mind, and what we see on the page are the written remains of that vision.

Harlan Ellison has said, "It's easy to become a writer; it's hard to stay a writer." One way to stay a writer is to participate in a writers' group. By doing so you are making a commitment to your writing and your creative life. Writing is hard work, and it helps to be in community with other writers who respect and support the commitment you've made to your craft. The Written Remains Writers Group has always been open to writers at all levels of experience, as well as writers working in a variety of categories, and you will find that diversity represented in this anthology.

A writer who presents his or her work to public scrutiny has committed an act of bravery. A willingness to let others read your work is an important step in a writer's creative journey. This anthology is representative of the creative journeys of eight people who have made a commitment to "stay writers."

JM Reinbold, Founder and Director
The Written Remains Writers Group
Wilmington, Delaware
21 June 2007

CONTENTS

AT SEA

RAMONA
DEFELICE-LONG

The air thunders above him and he slides, feet first, into the cold of the ocean. Had he thought about it, the cold would have been shocking. He had always imagined the ocean as warm. Here most of all, where the sun shone bright and brutal through every long day, the water should be something other than frigid.

In the movies, on the screen at the cavernous old theater at home, the water even looked warm. Waves lapped onto the shores of balmy Pacific Islands; native girls in the skimpiest costumes the Hayes Code would allow rushed, naive and friendly, to welcome handsome swashbucklers or the leering crew of the Bounty. It was hokey, but on the screen, back home, it all looked real.

The last movie he saw there, Fantasia, was nothing close to real. Later he'd thought, from something he had read or heard somewhere, that the ocean could be as strange and weird and colorful as what he had watched on the screen. He was not thinking about the ocean, though, while looking at Fantasia. He was not thinking at all, in the back row with a girl who, because soon he was leaving, off to war, to be a hero, decided yes, she must love him.

But he thought of it later, looking down at the ocean. If asked, which he never was, he would have said the water was warm, because on the screen, the waves looked as warm as girls.

And so, on this day, another with blazing sun bouncing off the dark blue plate-glassy calm surface, the water is a shock. Not that it is so very cold, or even cold at all. In fact, had he tried, he could not even call it chilled. There is only the absence of the warmth he would have expected.

It rushes over him, swiftly, feet to head. Always feet first—he has never learned to dive. Some of the other guys have gone for swims off the ship, secretly, when they were in port or the officers were meeting. They dove off the side and swam, sometimes briefly and quietly, just to get away with it, sometimes drunk and raucous, to show they have no fear. He has never tried, not for either reason. Swimming off the ship is off limits, and he is not a rule breaker. Whether he likes them or not, whether they make some sense or none, he obeys orders. It is what makes him a good soldier.

HE DRIFTS slowly, gently upheld by the currents running just below the surface. He always loved to float on his back, face to the sun, watching the sky—that was pure pleasure. Swimming—stroking and kicking, holding your breath, using up energy—that was work. Diving took skill and swimming took effort. If he wanted to work, he used to tell his older brother Kevin, he would dig potatoes.

Kevin had taught him how to swim. Kevin insisted he learn and made him practice. Everyone should be able to save himself, Kevin had said. So he learned, more to please Kevin than anything else. Because of it, he can swim to save himself, but he has never enjoyed it. Floating, though, he always loved, from the very first time he buoyed up.

Summer afternoons, after chores, he and Kevin would rush to their swimming hole. The water there was freezing, always, and deep and dark. Two huge rocks hung over the pool and kept half of it shadowed and chilly. Kevin liked to dive from the rocks, his straight lean body disappearing into the black water until he splashed up, yelping, laughing. Kevin tried and tried to teach him to dive, but he could never learn. Even now, if he tries, he can pull up a memory of those efforts, the fierce sting of the water on his stomach, the whoosh of air rushing from his lungs when he hit with a belly flop. If he ever needed to save someone, he would tell Kevin, he'd just jump in. Diving is not a requirement.

The swimming hole was part of an old quarry outside of town. The quarries were why there was a town at all. Their dad had worked there as a young man, carving out blocks of stone for a canal company. There were five or six quarries to work and strong young men came to work in them. The work was hot and hard and dangerous, but a man could make a living. If he didn't get killed doing it, that is.

Then the company had enough of the stone. In '21, the quarries were closed and filled with water. The strong young men drifted away. Some looked for other stone deposits to harvest. Some, like his dad, stayed close and grew oats without ever once forgetting that oats weren't what drew him.

His dad talked, every day, about the quarries. The two brothers listened, fascinated, admiring, staring at their father's wide shoulders and thick arms and the little scars from flying bits of rock that peppered his face and forearms.

There was no feeling, Father said, like busting rock with a pickaxe. You felt the shocks from your hands to your feet and, after a while, your arms went completely numb and your jaw locked tight. The only feeling left was in your toes. Father said he would wiggle his toes in their steel-tipped boots between every hit just to find a part of himself that was still pliable. That felt alive.

Father had left the quarry before it shut down. Something happened one day, not long before the company pulled out, and he walked away, never to return to stone breaking. He never said what had happened. He never said if it had happened to him. He only said the same thing, in the exact same way: "One day, something happened and I walked away and never went back."

He'd saved his money, so he bought a farm nearby and got lucky. He said so, time and time again. He got lucky. He had found good land nearby and then a good woman to marry and then sired two good sons. This land would be theirs, he promised. He taught his boys to nurture the bit of earth he had purchased. He taught them to find life in the soil and not to live, numbed, by splitting up stone. But they never listened as hard to his advice about farming as they did to his stories about breaking stone.

And he forbade his sons to swim at the quarry. They were good boys, generally, but on this they disobeyed. Not their father's orders or the "mystery" of the something that had happened kept them from sneaking off to swim. They kept suits hidden in a tree nook and dried off before they came home. The hole at the quarry was off limits, but the brothers didn't listen. At home, orders didn't seem so important. On your own land, even your father's rules were easy to break.

AT NIGHT, in their twin beds under the eaves, Kevin told him stories. The beginnings were different but the same—a kid wandered from his parents, a kid snuck off to play, a kid ran away in the middle of chores— but the kid always ended up the same way: floating in the quarry. In the dark, Kevin's spook stories made good listening, but they were never very frightening. He knew with sure and utter clarity, even when he was too young to understand sure and utter clarity, that Kevin would never do anything to hurt him. That included trying to scare him to death. So he understood that these were Kevin's not-so-clever inventions. Kevin was lying about the kids in the quarry. Older brothers always told scary stories. It was simply entertainment, a way to pass time in the dark.

But sometimes, as he drifted atop the quarry water, a vine or a fallen tree branch brushed against him, and a thrill shot through his cold body. He would let his feet drop and he would tread a while and let his mind wander towards the unthinkable what if. What would he do, really, really do, if a lifeless hand or bloated head popped up to the surface beside him?

He had only ever seen one drowned body. It was at the beach, on the Atlantic, where they had gone the summer after their baby sister was born. The baby was a surprise, a surprise of a sister, born to a mother everyone thought much too old to be having another child. He heard those comments, in school, at church, in town at the feed store, as if his parents had done something wrong, as if this coming baby was something wrong.

It scared him in a way that was new. Kevin's stories never scared him. His father's "something happened" never scared him. But this, this dangerous baby growing inside his too-old mother gave him nightmares. And he was not alone. At night, he heard his father pacing on the porch, back and forth, as if the pattern of his footsteps could hold off the worrying. His mother worked all day, long and hard as farm wives do, but having a baby was a different kind of work, and far more dangerous, but in an inexplicable way. Like breaking stone in the quarry had been for his father.

His mother did fine. The baby was fine. And out of the blue, as celebration, Father said they should go to the ocean. They had never seen the ocean! he declared, and they should. In fact, they'd never had a family vacation before; they could never leave the farm. But now Kevin was eighteen, out of school, old enough to stay behind and watch the crops. He offered to. Go, he'd urged them. Take the baby. See the ocean. He didn't mind missing, this time. He'd go next time. He had his whole life to see the ocean.

They went. They left Kevin to mind the farm, and they took the baby to see the ocean.

He was amazed. The beach was amazing: the sand, the breeze, the waves. The ocean had so much energy and power, and the water was so warm. He stood on the edge of the water and watched, wave in, wave out, over and over until the sun dipped below the line of the horizon. The first three days, he stayed all day. He could have stayed forever.

The next day, the fourth of their vacation, a squall blew in, and that was even better. The waves were white-capped and blasted onto the shore. They hurtled shells and sea creatures around the sand and he gathered up all kinds of things he never knew existed, then washed them carefully and held them up before his baby sister so she could grab them with her new, fat little hands.

Later, the water grew calm again. The sand that had been churned up settled and the water turned blue-green, but colder. The storm had made it cold. He went out floating, and it was almost like home, warm face and cold back. Something brushed against him, touching his bottom and his heels, and he popped his feet down, just like at home, to look around. But it wasn't a tree branch or a vine, and he was just curious. He wasn't scared at all.

"I swam through some fish!" he yelled to his mother. She was under an umbrella they had rented, holding the baby out of the sun. He was far out and she couldn't possibly have understood him, but she waved at him and he was delighted. It was the only way to describe his feeling, surrounded by the warm water and the curious fish. He was delighted. He couldn't wait to tell Kevin.

And then, a cry came from up the beach. It quickly turned into a scream.

His mother's head whipped sharply towards it, and for one second, he quit treading and went under. He opened his eyes, but the fish were gone. Salt stung his eyeballs. He surfaced with a gasp. The cries were there again, louder, and so he caught his breath and swung his body flat, face down, and swam the way he hated, fast and hard and purposeful, the way Kevin had taught him, to save his life.

He sliced through the water to the shore. He stumbled in with the incoming waves, sucking in enough extra air to holler at his mother to stay there, under the umbrella. He was surprised when she obeyed. Where was his father? He didn't know. He didn't pause to wonder.

He ran towards the cries. The air was cold on his skin as he skirted the waves to join a small crowd gathered near one of the fishing piers built from the sand into the water. His teeth were chattering when he got close. His fingers were blue, he noticed, as he wrapped his arms around himself and looked down at what had caused the crying.

It was a body, the body of a boy, and bent over it was Father.

The boy had washed up against the pilings of the pier. Some ladies hoping to find seashells had found this, a boy's body, instead. They screamed, and Father had come running.

Father pressed on the boy's gray chest. He put his ear down towards the boy's mouth. There was no point. There was no life in this body. Father's movements were all an act, an act of kindness, or something like it. There was no life left to save, but it would be cruel not to pretend to try.

He moved through the crowd to be near his father. Shivering, he knelt in the sand beside him. His knee slid in the sand and touched the boy's side. Father shook his head, first at him, then at the boy's body.

Father's face looked tight and furious. He'd never seen his father look that way; he'd never seen his father look helpless before. That's when he figured it out, right there on the sand next to the boy's body. He knew the "something" that had happened at the quarry.

That night, the local police came to their hotel room and told them the story. Four boys had gone sailing, the day before, just before the squall blew in. Their boat had capsized in the water, miles away. The other three had washed up not far from one another, but the fourth had not. The storm must have driven him away from the others, the officer said. His voice shook; his eyes looked red. Father shook his head again, saying nothing.

They left the beach the next morning, driving towards the farm, hardly stopping. They did not speak of the drowning, but only spoke of the sand and the breeze and how much the baby liked reaching for the seashells. They repeated it all when they reached home, to Kevin, as if that was all that had happened.

He waited until nighttime, in the twin beds under the eaves, to tell Kevin about the boy. Kevin was astounded. He asked what the boy had looked like, but there was no way to describe it, even though he could still see the boy's face every time he closed his eyes and tried not to think about it.

"Did you touch him?" Kevin had asked.

He had nodded yes, into the darkness of the room.

"How did he feel?" Kevin had asked.

He closed his eyes and did not answer until Kevin said his name again. He saw the body and his knee sliding through the sand towards it.

"Cold," he finally answered. "He felt cold."

HE NEVER went back to swim in the quarry. Kevin was surprised when he refused the first time, but he never said anything to tease him about it. It was getting near to autumn, anyway, and too cold for swimming.

"Maybe next summer," Kevin had said.

But the next summer, Kevin was gone.

He was one of the first boys in town to enlist, the morning after Pearl Harbor. He left the farm when it was still dark on Monday, the day after the bombing. He borrowed Father's pickup, stopped on the way for two friends, and the three of them drove into town to join the army.

In a few weeks, no time at all it felt like, Kevin was gone for training. It was the only time, other than sleepovers at friends' houses and the beach trip that the two brothers had ever spent nights away from one another.

"Two more years and you can come with me," Kevin had promised.

"Two more years, and the war will be over," he had answered.

It wasn't. When he turned eighteen, he hadn't seen his brother in over a year. Kevin wrote from North Africa. Don't come here, his letters said in the crude code they had once, as kids, developed. The code was simple; he was surprised the censors didn't black it out. Then he decided they just hadn't bothered. What was the danger in Kevin's message?

Don't come here, Kevin's code warned him. There's no water.

No water. He'd read the code and told Father he was joining the Navy instead of the Army. The decision was upsetting to his parents. The chance that he might meet up with Kevin was slight, but didn't he want to take it? Didn't he want the chance, any chance, to see his brother?

He did not tell them it had nothing to do with Kevin. The water in the Pacific, he was certain, would be warmer.

He became a gunner. He shot at airplanes, sometimes only one or two, sometimes what looked like entire squadrons. Sometimes, when the fighting got hot, spent shells flew out and hit his face and arms and helmet, leaving little burn marks, little scars, that peppered his face and forearms.

Only once did he ever write about what he saw or experienced in battle. It was not in code, and it was not to Kevin. He wrote it to his father.

Sometimes, he wrote, when his gun fired steady without pausing, his hands grew numb from the vibrations. And so did his arms and shoulders and everywhere else, except his toes, which he wriggled inside his boots just to make sure a part of him was still pliable. To make sure he was still alive.

Was this what you meant, he wrote to his father, about splitting the stone in the quarry?

HE WILL never know the answer.

It thunders again, above the water, and another body breaks the surface, frightening off a school of fish that skittered away just a minute ago, when his own bound feet pierced their grouping. Now they swim away from Hazelton, a boy from out west, California. Hazelton had blond hair, pretty hair that he wore longish. Last night, it was matted with blood, blood that dissolves now as the strands sway in the water. Soon, sharks will smell the blood and come. Someone should have washed it.

In the medical unit, he and Hazelton were put in beds next to one another. Hazelton had a gash across his scalp and, more seriously, a stomach wound. It kept him moaning into the night until early morning. Not long after, his own sounds grew shriller and then silent. Last night, though, he had tried hard not to make any sounds. Hazelton's moans had reminded him of something. It took him a while to recognize it, to filter the familiar sound through all the strange new noises he had never wanted to learn. In a quick moment of quiet, he places the sound. Hazelton's moans are just like the creaking of the shutters of his and Kevin's windows when the wind blew past, southbound.

He opens his eyes, just the barest of slits, expecting to be home.

He is not. He does not see the hospital. He only sees the sound.

The gauze wrapped around the top of his head and most of his body makes a scraping sound on the pillow as he slowly, slowly rotates his head to look at the bed beside him.

The moaning sound stops. It is day, but the room is dark and growing darker. He still has a little bit of sight. He uses it to stare at a face he knows as clearly as the sound. It is the face of the boy on the beach.

Something happened, he realizes.

Something happened. And he'll never go back.

Hazelton slips silently through the water, turning over and over and over, gradually drifting closer, almost within reach. At the last moment, something in the current catches and grabs, and Hazelton pulls away. His blond hair, clean and golden, swirls like a crown around his face. Or a halo. The current cannot hold them. The water grows colder as they drift down, feet first, falling together beyond the last reaches of light. They face each other in the dark cold water, and then drop down.

Baffled
by the
Green Door

Sherry Thompson

The door closes, and I turn and walk down the steps. As I start walking in the direction Marcea's mom pointed, I remember words unheeded or perhaps words I didn't want to hear at the time. The Girl Scout troop was to meet here, and then bike over to the roller rink. Our troop leader said Marcea's was the closest to the rink. I knew that. I should have known they were already gone.

Mrs. Brown knows I don't have a bike. I told her when the troop was planning the trip to the roller rink. Maybe that's why Marcea's mom looked so disapproving. Or, was she angry? Impatient? I'm not sure. I spent the time she was talking to me trying to read her face, and I spend more time now trying to understand what I saw. I stick with my first guess. Mrs. Brown told us we would bike over to the rink, so I shouldn't have knocked at the door and asked her where everyone was. That was why she looked like she did.

I stop and sit on the grass, and look for four-leafed clovers. My fingers explore the plants one by one, but I am still thinking about the situation. I want to be with the rest of my troop. Right now, they're together in the bright magic place of "The Rink." I've never been to a rink. I've heard about them. I conjure a picture of bright lights and laughter.

Then I remember the skating part, and I get confused. Why do I care? I don't know how to skate. The skates I've dropped beside me are used, but not by me. They're from Goodwill, the huge store up the steep hill in Wilmington. I've had my skates for a year maybe, but I can't use them because I can't keep my balance.

The same was true with the bike I got for my birthday. Training wheels were on it and Daddy was eager to raise them so I could balance. But I couldn't balance. I tried every day after school for a week. I was scared and confused. Why couldn't I balance? Everyone else did it.

At the end of the week, the bike was gone. Mommy and Daddy explained that the doctor had found out, and told them to take it back. I had rheumatic fever and German measles before I was one year old. I almost died of them. Now my heart is scarred and it murmurs. I know the words - have known them for years and can glibly pass them on to teachers. It means I can't exercise hard because it hurts my heart. That's why I don't take gym.

But the doctor had said once -- I'd heard him say it -- "She could dig ditches. That was years ago, and she's fine now. .... Okay, I'll write a new note."

The doctor must have changed his mind about my heart. Somehow he had found out about the bike, and then he'd changed his mind and warned my parents to take the bike back. I wonder briefly how he found out about it. I am almost relieved that he did. I couldn't balance and, after a week, I'd grown tired of trying.

An old Packard is racing toward my corner, its radio blaring, "Don't know what they're doing, but they laugh a lot...wish they'd let me in." The tires screech as the sedan takes a wide loop to make it around the corner. The next line of "The Green Door" I hear is, "Door slammed, hospitality's thin there." I repeat the new lyrics carefully, until I've got them memorized. They make me think of Marcea's mom.

I get up from the grassy spot with two new four-leafed clovers. We have lots in the neighborhood. Mr. McDaniel says we have experimental grass. I don't care. I'm just glad to have two more four-leafed clovers for my grandfather's New Testament. It is already stuffed and it's getting hard to find empty pages. I put the tiny leaves in my rumpled handkerchief and slide it carefully back into my pocket.

Picking up the skates, I start toward home, then stop and walk toward the shopping center. At home, I'd have to explain why I'm not with the troop, but I'm not sure I know the answer. Besides, home would be someone arguing, or Uncle Dan smelling funny, or maybe Mommy would be having a headache. My spirits lift a little. I don't need to be home right now. They don't know everyone left without me.

As I walk, I try to understand. I spend a lot of time trying to understand why things happen differently for me. I already know one reason. Mommy has explained it to me many times. Our neighbors and my friends are OPs - "other people." They aren't like us. That's her explanation, but I don't understand that either. They look like us. Of course, they have stuff and they go places. But they look like us. Why are their lives so different? Why am I different? Why didn't the troop leader remember that I don't have a bike? Why did Marcea's mom look disapproving? Have I done something? I told the troop leader about not having a bike. I really did. The gleam of the rink fun disappears, swallowed by a surge of guilt and hurt.

It wouldn't have been fun. Don't I know that by now? It's never fun with them. Even my best friends, Mary and Diana, aren't fun when they are part of the troop. They are all the same, all OPs, all the same except for Hazel and me. That is why I am the one who sits with Hazel while they have the scout meetings. Hazel can't talk properly and she hits. I wonder who is sitting with Hazel at the rink. Maybe … I'm lost for an answer. No one else ever sits with Hazel. She hurts, after all.

Brookside Boulevard brings my thoughts back to my feet. A horn blares as a car flashes by. I want to call out angrily that I was stopped, but it's gone and other cars are taking its place. I try to decide what store I will go to after I cross. I have twenty cents and I need notebook paper, so I should go to the five and ten. But first, I want to look in some of the other stores. I find an opening in the traffic and hurry to the middle of the road, then dart forward again, nearly tripping on the curb as I jump up to it. I can feel the soft throb of my heart, and I wonder what part of the sound is the rheumatic fever murmur I've had since I was one.

Girl Scouts are still on my mind, though. I decide to go to the department store first, and peek at the things in the Girl Scout display. I push through the glass double doors, so heavy I can barely open them, then slip along the wall past the rows of clothing. Juniors and Misses look boring, with all the same colors on each rack. At Goodwill, the colors are all different on the racks. Everyone at school is wearing brown and tan and a funny green right now, just like the clothing I'm passing. I'm wearing red and a very dark purple. Yesterday, I wore yellow...

Salesgirl. I slip around a rack of blouses and retreat toward the wall. I look for an opening to go to the escalator. Now. I hurry over and stand at the top, trying to get over the familiar terror. One foot lifts, but my mind says not now. I wait, as step after step glides away from me. I try again. I feel a nudge from behind and stumble onto a downward-drifting step, my heart racing. I'm scared and mad. That wasn't nice. But now the bottom is approaching and I hastily ready myself, so I don't get pushed again.

No one is at the Girl Scout display. The skinny, grouchy sales lady is with two women at the fancy food stuff. I squat down and look through the heavy glass at the badge display. When will my badges come? I love them. They are so beautiful - tiny miracles of satiny sewing. I've earned that one and that one, and that one over there.

The knot-tying one was my favorite. I used twine to tie all my knots and then glued each one to its own half sheet of notebook paper. Labeling them all carefully in my neatest cursive, I'd twisted the left corners of the pages to hold them together and given them to Mrs. White five months ago. She had made complimentary sounds, and I had smiled.

I wonder why mine are taking so long. Everyone else's sashes are covered with five and six or more badges. I have my pin but that's all. I wonder what badge to work on next. I've done just about all of the ones that I understand. Sewing stuff is out. No one in my family sews. Other badges mean going to other places to do them -- like the horse-riding. I stand up.

Horses. Someday I'll have a horse. I'll live in Ocean City and have a horse in a barn and I'll teach math in junior high like Mr. Fenstermacher. He's a nice man. He told my parents I should go to college, and that made everyone angry. I'll grade my tests out on the music pier. I'll get a big shell to weigh down the papers so they won't fly away in the wind.

"May I help you?" Strange how the woman's face seems to say instead, "What are -you- doing here?"

I stammer, "I'm just looking at my badges."

"You'll have to bring your mother and the troop leader's paper if you want to buy them."

I look at her in puzzlement but I don't ask anything. She wants me to leave, and I want me to leave. I oblige us both. The badges will come - someday. I'll be getting a bunch - all in little boxes and bits of tissue. In the meantime, the escalator is too close for comfort. I dodge away, letting several people speed up the silver stair, then creep carefully onto the bottom step. It's easier going up - no gulf gaping below my feet.

I walk toward the five and ten, checking my money carefully on the way. Twenty cents. Two nickels and a dime. All I have left of my twenty-five cent allowance. I bought a Hershey bar with one nickel. It must be nice to get dollars like some kids do. Then you can get toys and stuff.

Cookie-selling season is coming soon. Maybe I'll sell lots of cookies and win a prize. I've wanted one of the fortune-telling black balls ever since they showed us the prizes last year. But I only sold five boxes last spring. Some of the girls sold fifty or more. They said their mothers helped, and their fathers took boxes to work. It isn't fair. Why don't my parents help? Daddy works. Why doesn't he sell boxes? But this year will be different. I'll walk all over Brookside. I'll stop at every door. Or, not. I hate trying to sell cookies. Everyone looks at me just like Marcea's mom did. But I'll do it. Maybe I'll do it. By then, maybe I'll be braver.

I open the door of the five and ten to the sound of "Green Door." It's just starting! Trying to crack the code, I listen to the words carefully.

"Green door. What's that secret you're keepin'?
Watching til the morning comes creeping..."

What -was- behind the green door? Maybe that's where OPs live.

I find the notepaper and sigh. The icky paper with the wide-spaced lines is fifteen cents and the good paper is twenty-five. I shouldn't have bought that candy bar. I don't want the icky paper. Tears in my eyes, I pick up the icky paper and then put it down. I feel the coins in my pocket, feeling, hoping, wishing for another coin to appear. It doesn't.

Someone is coming -- the old guy who owns the store. I don't leave. He's nice.

"What's wrong?"

I blink back tears and shake my head.

He persists. 'Something's wrong. What is it?"

I force the words out, "I don't have enough for the good paper." I reach into my pocket, scattering the handkerchief and a clover to the ground, and bring out the three coins. The other clover comes out too, sitting on the base of my thumb.

"Yeah, but look! You've got a four-leaf clover there!"

I shrug. He might as well have said I was breathing.

"Tell you what. I'll buy the clover from you for a nickel. Then you'll have enough for the college-ruled."

I stare a moment to make sure he's serious. His warm brown eyes stare back from his crinkled face. Other thoughts flit and are dismissed. What will my grandfather say? I won't tell. They'll never know. Mommy will have a headache or something, and they'll never know. Elation floods me, but I hold it in, taking care first that I've covered everything. I'll come in through the carport. I'll hide the bag when I come in the door. I'll put the paper into my notebook when no one is looking. And it will be the good paper. I nod.

"Deal." He smiles and waves me to the register by the wall.

As he rings up the sale, "Green Door" ends on the radio,

"-- someone laughed out loud behind the green door.
All I want to do is join the happy crowd behind the green door."

I'd forgotten to listen to the rest of the words. I still don't know what is behind the green door. The man hands me the slim brown bag and picks up the clover from the counter with a moist fingertip. As he studies it, I ask, "What's behind the green door?"

He glances at me and shakes his head. Then, turning back, he rests his forearms on the countertop and studies me. His eyes are kindly still, and I don't mind. "Kid, the boy in that song would be real disappointed if he ever got inside that door. It's like the grass is greener, ya'know? Nothing special, except imagining."

I nod, sort of getting it. He nods back and grins. "Good. Enjoy your paper!" Then he walks away.

I start for home, imagining how I'll use the first sheet of paper. Probably I'll draw a horse - the one I'll have in Ocean City. And I can write down all the words I know from that song. Maybe I'll see a clue. The five and ten guy is wrong. There is something special behind the green door. The singer knows this, and so do I. Someday, I'll find out what it is, and why the door is shut.

CHRISTMAS SURPRISE

JACQUIE JUERS

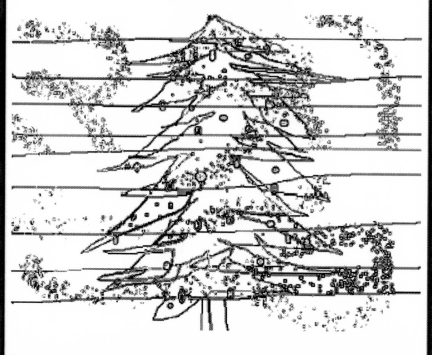

Gretchen Hall kicked the snow with the toe of her ugly black rubber boot and stared at the ground while Billy Jenkins continued chanting, "Cry baby, cry baby. What'cha gonna do? Better stop crying, Santa's watching. Go on, run home crying to Mommy."

She kicked the snow even harder and a chunk of ice flew off, hitting Billy in the knee. He howled in surprise and pain before he leapt at Gretchen. She'd crossed a line by fighting back, even though she didn't mean to do it. Billy shoved her down in the snow and pushed her face down in a drift. Gretchen flailed her feet and twisted around in order to breathe. One of her mittens came off in the struggle and she was able to scratch at Billy. It wasn't long before other kids were surrounding them, chanting, "Fight, fight, fight," and then it wasn't long before the policeman on the corner who helped them cross the street was pulling them apart.

"She started it," Billy yelled. "She kicked snow and some ice hit me in the knee."

Officer Paulsen held them both by the scruff of their coats. Gretchen's hair was plastered to her head and her nose was bleeding where Billy had rubbed it into an ice patch. He hadn't gotten off scot-free though. There was a scratch down one side of his cheek.

"Is that true, Gretchen?"

"I didn't mean to. He was teasing me and I kicked some snow. I didn't even know there was any ice in it." Gretchen tried to keep her voice steady and not whine. No matter what, she was in for it now. Officer Paulsen would tell her mother when she saw him on the corner the next morning on her way to work.

It wasn't fair. She would get in trouble. She always got in trouble when the other kids teased her. Her mother didn't understand. Besides, it was all her mother's fault. Just a week ago her mother had said that Santa Claus did exist and he brought the tree and all the presents.

It was only two days before Christmas and Gretchen couldn't help but notice that everyone else already had their Christmas tree. She could see them glowing in the windows of houses she passed on her way home from school. The lights shimmering through the snow looked so magical. Even when Santa brought the tree to Gretchen's house, no one could see it from the outside because she lived in a poky, little apartment above Hank's Meat Market. No one else lived on Main Street in the city. Everyone else in school had one of the big white houses that Gretchen walked past everyday. They all had fathers, too. Gretchen's father didn't live with them, that's why they couldn't have one of the big houses. Gretchen didn't know why, she just knew that her mother coughed whenever anyone said anything about her ex-husband and refused to be in the room when Gretchen's father came to pick her up every other weekend.

"I don't care who started this," Officer Paulsen said. "This isn't anyway to behave, especially two days before Christmas. Now go on, both of you. Get on home." He gave both of them a nudge on the back, sending them in opposite directions. Gretchen plodded down the street, passing stores advertising, "Indulge yourself." Or, "First metal toys since before the war."

She stopped in Hank's to pick up the key to the apartment. Her mother would be working. That was another thing that was different. Nobody else's mother worked. They visited the classroom and brought treats for their child's birthday and Christmas and Halloween. Gretchen's birthday was the end of January. Hank always gave her some day old things from the bakery next door to take to school, but everyone knew that Gretchen's mother didn't make them.

It would be many years before Gretchen would understand that her mother was just as embarrassed by these things as Gretchen was or that the only way Gretchen's mother could afford a Christmas tree was to wait until Christmas Eve when she could get a tree for fifty cents. Even when she figured these things out, it wouldn't make Gretchen feel any better, and it certainly didn't help the ten-year-old girl with blood running down her face, trying not to cry.

"What's 'a matter?" Hank asked when he saw Gretchen.

"Billy Jenkins was teasing me because I said Santa Claus would bring our tree. He says there is no Santa Claus. Why did my mother tell me a lie that makes people tease me?" The tears that had been threatening overflowed, and Gretchen started crying in earnest, angry with herself for doing it. She was too big to be standing in the meat market bawling like a baby, but Hank didn't seem to mind.

"I think somebody needs cocoa, and I was just about to have some myself. You come on with me." Hank guided Gretchen to the back room where he took her coat and said, "Go on, wash your face while I pour the cocoa."

"It'll hurt," Gretchen said.

"You have to do it sometime, may as well be now. Will you have two marshmallows or three?"

"Four please," Gretchen said. It was a routine they went through whenever they had cocoa.

When Gretchen came out of the bathroom, the cocoa was ready.

"I gave you an extra marshmallow for the bloody nose," Hank said. "Did it ever occur to you that maybe Santa Claus exists for some people and not for others?"

"How can that be?" Gretchen tilted her head, as she did whenever someone presented her with a new idea. It was almost like the new idea went into one part of her brain and unbalanced her head for a minute until it settled down and her head returned to equilibrium.

"Maybe, just maybe, mind you, Santa Claus is more of an idea than a real person. Maybe Santa Claus is the desire to make people happy and it doesn't sound like this Billy Jenkins has any of that in him. So, for him, Santa Claus doesn't exist. Maybe, people like your mother, who are just trying to do the best they can to make everything as normal as possible, have Santa Claus inside of them."

Gretchen hid her face behind the large mug of hot chocolate. Here he went again. Hank told her frequently how tough her mother had it and how hard she tried to give Gretchen everything she wanted; but she didn't, did she?

Gretchen thought of the wallpaper in her room. Sure, she got what she wanted, but she'd never heard of any of her classmates having to peel the old wallpaper off the wall before they could get the new stuff put up. Her mother said it was just so she would have time to think about the wallpaper she'd picked out, but she could have done that without chapping her hands in bleach water and scraping her knuckles on the wall to get the old paper off.

"Either he's real or he isn't," Gretchen said. "If he's a real person then Billy Jenkins is wrong. If he isn't a real person, then my mother lied to me."

"Do you believe your mother would lie to you?"

Later in life, in her therapist's office Gretchen, would reconsider that question and wonder about her answer, but under Hank's steely glare all she could do was shake her head, and hide her face behind her mug.

"I have to go clean up. You finish that cocoa and get upstairs. If you want Christmas decorations so much, you could make some of your own. I haven't seen any snowflakes you've made or paper chains."

"We don't have any colored paper." Gretchen would never admit this to any of her schoolmates, but Hank was safe. He wouldn't tell anyone.

"You've got crayons, right?" Gretchen nodded. "You tear off a sheet of the butcher paper on your way out the door and you can color what ever you want on it."

It didn't sound very festive to Gretchen, but Hank was trying to be nice and she didn't have anything else to do when she got upstairs. There wasn't any homework now that Christmas vacation had started. Hank left and Gretchen finished her cocoa, thinking about what Hank said about Santa Claus and her mother. Even he hadn't really answered the question, though it sounded like he said that Santa Claus was an idea not a person, which Gretchen could believe more easily than a man with flying reindeer who went to every house in the world in one night. She would have to stay awake the next night and see who it was that decorated their house.

Gretchen climbed the long flight of stairs in the hallway next to the meat market. In the afternoon gloom, the apartment was cold and dark. Gretchen fiddled with a knob on the side of the oil stove in the middle of the living room. No one else had some ugly stove, but it was the only heat in the apartment so Gretchen couldn't ignore it. She turned on a lamp and tuned the radio to a popular music station. Her mother would turn it off as soon as she got home, but until then, Gretchen could revel in the music and pretend she was like everyone else.

The roll of butcher paper from Hank was on the sofa where she'd thrown it. That wasn't the worst idea in the world. She could make some paper chains and festoon them around the apartment and maybe a couple of snowflakes for her bedroom window. Her room was slightly more cheerful because the light from the town's Christmas decorations on the lampposts shone through, another first. During the war there had been a blackout and Gretchen could barely remember how bright the decorations made the room.

She got out her crayons and thought about how she'd decorate the chains. She couldn't change the color of the paper because she didn't want to use up her crayons trying to color every inch of the paper. Then she remembered the magazines and catalogs. There was a special pile in the hall for Gretchen to cut up and make paper dolls out of, but she could just cut colorful things out and glue them to the brown paper.

Gretchen snipped brown paper strips and colorful squares out of magazines. When everything was lined up, she went to the kitchen and mixed some flour and water with a pinch of salt to make paste. While she was engaged in this messy process her mother came home from work. Gretchen could see that she was ready to say something about the mess, but Gretchen ignored the look and said, "I'm making some chains to put up around the house. That way Santa Claus won't have so much work tomorrow night."

"I'll start dinner. I have some eggs, and I thought I'd make pancakes tonight."

Gretchen tried to be positive. "That's good." Pancakes for dinner was another thing that set her apart. Everyone knew they were breakfast food, but on the rare occasions Gretchen had them, it was for dinner. It was another revelation Gretchen would have later in life. Her mother not only didn't have time to make pancakes in the morning because she had to go to work, but it was a very inexpensive dinner.

The evening passed with Gretchen's mother not saying anything and Gretchen ignoring the unspoken disapproval. Christmas Eve morning was no different except that Gretchen didn't have to go to school. Her mother had already left for work when she got up and Gretchen went down to the meat market. She knew Hank could use some help with deliveries and packaging meat for other people's Christmas dinners. It gave her something to do and then her mother wouldn't feel like it was charity when Hank gave them a roast or a ham for Christmas, which he did every year.

Before Gretchen knew it, she'd collected $4.00 in tips for deliveries and it was time to lock the store. Hank handed her a parcel and said, "Tell your mother, Merry Christmas. The snowflakes in your window look great."

Gretchen knew it would be spaghetti for supper tonight. She walked past the door to the apartment and went to look in the window of Tyndell's Drug Store. Lights sparkled on the tinsel, and cotton batting was mounded to look like snow. Gretchen could see Mr. Tyndell, so she tried the door.

"I'm sorry, we're closing...Oh, hello, Gretchen. Are you ready for Christmas?"

"I guess so. I don't have much to do. Santa does everything tonight after I go to bed."

"What about your mother? Did you get her anything?"

"No." This was something new. None of the kids at school ever talked about buying anything for their mothers, but then they had fathers who would do that. Gretchen tried to remember if her mother ever opened anything on Christmas morning. It seemed there were a couple of items from Santa for her as well. "Santa leaves her a couple of presents, too. What could I get her?"

"Well, I'm about to close, but we can take a quick look and see what there is. What about a scarf? I have these nice ones with poinsettias, or there's this pin." Mr. Tyndell pointed to a gold tree shaped pin with sparkly stones.

It was the most beautiful thing Gretchen had ever seen and she immediately pictured it on the collar of her mother's coat when she went to church on Christmas day.

"I'll take it," Gretchen said, but her face immediately fell. "I only have $4.00."

Mr. Tyndell looked at the bottom of the box and Gretchen could see the price plainly: $5.00.

"Lucky for you it's on sale."

"It's not marked," Gretchen said.

"I haven't done it yet, but no one will buy it after Christmas so I can sell it to you for $2.50, and I'll even throw in a chocolate bar for you." He rang it all into the register and handed it to Gretchen along with a small piece of wrapping paper. "This is a scrap. Wrap it up while I turn off the lights and we'll both go home for Christmas."

As Gretchen wrapped, Mr. Tyndell pointed to a bow that was on the floor.

"Stick that on top."

Gretchen turned left out the door and Mr. Tyndell turned right.

"Merry Christmas," he said. "I noticed you do some deliveries for Hank."

Gretchen nodded.

"I don't have a lot, but maybe in the new year you could start doing some for me. I'll pay you, say, 25¢ per delivery."

"That would be nice. You don't have to pay me though. I don't have anything to do in the afternoons."

"You should learn now, Gretchen, that it's important to be paid for the jobs you do." Gretchen nodded.

The stairs didn't seem as dark or cold as she headed up to the apartment. Her mother had beaten her home.

"Where have you been?"

"I was helping Mr. Tyndell after I finished at the meat market." Gretchen handed the butcher wrapped paper package to her mother. The other small package was still in her coat pocket where she'd hidden it. She imagined how surprised her mother would be when she opened it the next morning. Gretchen would just have to be super sneaky in order to put it under the tree without her mother noticing.

"That's nice, but there's plenty to do for dinner here if you run out of things to do."

"He wants me to do deliveries for him after school starting in January. He says he doesn't have that many, and he'll pay me fifteen cents for each delivery." Gretchen hadn't planned to lie; the number just came out of her mouth.

Her mother looked at her and Gretchen almost confessed. She felt the lie was written on her face. "You're too young to have a job."

"But I want to help you and be able to buy comic books or marbles sometimes."

"I don't want your school work to suffer."

"It won't; you'll see. He said he didn't have many deliveries."

Supper was a quiet meal, and afterwards they played Tiddlywinks. Gretchen's mother won, as usual, and Gretchen retreated to her room early. She'd gotten an extra large stack of books from the library, knowing that with school closed she'd have more time to read. Now the hard part, which book to read first? She ran her finger down the stack: Nancy Drew, too easy; a story about Lewis and Clark, not fun enough for Christmas Eve; a collection of short stories by O. Henry. That might be good. They'd read one in school and Gretchen liked it, and the stories were short so she could keep track of what went on in the living room. Gretchen started reading and laughed out loud at several of the stories.

At 9:00 her mother came in. "I brought you some peanut butter crackers and a hot water bottle. Get ready for bed. Santa can't come until you're asleep."

"How does he know if I'm asleep? I thought I just had to be in bed."

"He knows. He's Santa Claus."

"Some of the kids were teasing me that there is no Santa Claus."

Her mother nodded. "So that's what the fight was about. I heard about it on the way home. I wasn't going to talk about it until after tomorrow."

"Is there a Santa Claus? I have to know the truth. I get picked on enough. I don't want to get teased for things that I can do something about."

"That's why I wasn't going to talk about it until after tomorrow. Things aren't black and white, Gretchen. We'll talk about it tomorrow night. Go to sleep. We'll see what Santa Claus brings you."

"Night, Mother," Gretchen said, slipping a flannel nightgown over her head. She maneuvered out of her sweater in the tent made by the nightgown, then popped her head through and pulled off her stretch pants. Gretchen ran the hot water bottle around on the sheets to take the chill off, and then hopped into bed, curling her toes around the hot water bottle.

Gretchen closed her eyes, in case her mother checked on her, but under the blankets, she pinched herself every few minutes to stay awake. There would be awful bruises on her arms, but it was the only way to make sure she stayed awake. She listened, trying to hear any noises coming from the living room. It should have been easy. Christmas Eve was one of the few nights of the year that there was relatively little traffic on the street outside her window. The snow that began gently falling just after dark further muted any noises.

Wait! Gretchen's eyes opened. Was that the door at the bottom of the stairs? Gretchen lay perfectly still on her back, so that neither ear was muffled by the pillow. It must not have been, it never took anyone this long to climb the stairs. She thought about looking out the window to see if any cars were parked out front, but the bedsprings would creak and alert her mother. It must've been the street door because now she could hear her mother at the apartment door. Someone was definitely in the apartment.

Gretchen didn't have any problem staying awake for the next hour as she listened to snatches of activity from the front room. When she was sure that whoever was out there was involved in what they were doing, she eased herself out of bed. The room was frigid and Gretchen's teeth started chattering almost immediately. She crept to her bedroom door. She couldn't see the living room from the door, but there was a mirror on her mother's bedroom door across the hall and Gretchen had made sure it was positioned so she could see the living room in it before she went to bed.

A Christmas tree stood in the living room next to the side window. The lights twinkled and her mother was arranging glass balls. A sled was underneath with a big red bow, but that wasn't the best part. Later on, Gretchen regretted what she did, because "Santa Claus" never came on Christmas Eve again, but that night it didn't matter. Gretchen recognized the man putting the star on top of the tree. She burst out of her bedroom and ran straight into her father's arms.

COMPOST

MARY JO
DIANGELO

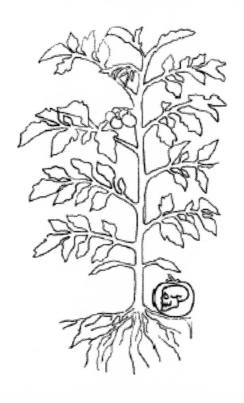

Priscilla never planned to become a gardener. But when her mother died, she inherited the flower garden along with the house. The first summer, Priscilla kept the garden going as a tribute to her mother, but planned to eventually plant it over with grass. Simple, easy grass.

But the flowers became the children Priscilla never had. And, like children, some rewarded her care with color and scent, others went bad for no good reason. By summer's end, Priscilla was hooked.

The next year she discovered composting. She hovered over the backyard pile of cabbage leaves and coffee grounds turning it with a pitchfork, gloating over the fat pink worms that transformed garbage into garden soil. But such odd things turned up in a compost pile: a rusted bangle bracelet, a cracked leather glove. How did such things get into her yard, Priscilla wondered?

By the third year, Priscilla's garden was bright with flowers, and the compost pile was waist high. That was the year the Bradys moved in next door.

Priscilla tried to be broadminded, but the Bradys reminded her of the discontented couples that visited the loan department of the bank where she worked. They spent too much money and fought about it when the bills came due. Priscilla thought that little Mrs. Brady spent too much time sunning herself in the backyard, exposing as much brown flesh as possible in a brief bikini. Unlike his wife, Mr. Brady never stopped moving. He prowled about the yard as though the chain link fence were a cage. He could relax more if his wife got a job, Priscilla thought, and then reminded herself it was none of her business.

ONE DAY Mr. Brady spoke to her over the fence as she was weeding her rose bed.

"Those sure are pretty flowers," he said.

Priscilla thanked him.

"You must be talented to grow flowers like that, especially the roses."

Modestly pleased, Priscilla protested that she hadn't gardened for long. Not really.

"You sure can't tell from looking at those roses," he said. "My wife loves roses."

Priscilla offered to cut a bouquet for him.

Mr. Brady thanked her. "She'd really like that."

"You know, I've wanted to ask you about that big dirt pile next to your shed."

"That's not dirt; it's compost," Priscilla explained as she cut the showiest blooms for Mrs. Brady. "I save all my vegetable scraps and shred all my newspapers. Then I dump them on the pile. In a few weeks, the microbes turn them into the best soil there is. That's why my flowers are so healthy."

"You mean bugs do all that?" he said. "They must be hungry."

"They are," Priscilla replied. "And compost piles are hot. That's what breaks things down so quickly."

"You don't say!"

Priscilla warmed to her favorite topic.

"At the Ag College, there's a compost pile not much bigger than mine. I know; I've seen it. Sometimes when a farm animal dies they bury it in the compost to see how fast it will decompose. Why, a 200 pound pig carcass disappeared in three weeks, bones and all."

"Bones and all. Now isn't that something," Mr. Brady murmured.

Priscilla suddenly felt he was laughing at her. You got your flowers, she thought. Now go away.

Handing him the bouquet, she said briskly, "There's a lot of information on the internet if you're really interested. Now I must get back to my weeding."

Priscilla was digging out a deep-rooted dandelion when the shouting began next door. Poor Mr. Brady. His attempt to please his wife had backfired.

"Thanks for nothing, Charlie," Mrs. Brady raged. "I saw you talking to that old maid. You're too cheap to buy me good roses, so you scrounge a few ratty flowers for free."

Outside, Priscilla's face burned. Really, the things you heard when people left their windows open. Imagine calling someone an old maid in this day and age. Inside, the Bradys continued to argue.

"These are nice roses. I thought you'd like them."

"You thought. You thought! Maybe if you stop thinking and start doing, things will get better around here. You made me promises, Charlie. A big house and all the best people. But look where I am - stuck here in this dirty old hole. Ouch! You didn't even take the thorns off. Now I'm bleeding."

Priscilla ducked as a door slammed and Mr. Brady stalked out into his backyard. Pacing back and forth, he muttered, "I'd like to give her a dirty old hole. About six feet under."

Priscilla shook her head. So many women didn't appreciate what they had. She felt a fierce, indignant anger at Mrs. Brady.

Not long after the flower incident, the Bradys erected a high stockade fence around their yard. Priscilla took no offense and planned to put trellises against the fence to support clematis and morning glory vines. She probably wants to sunbathe without even her miniscule bikini, she thought.

SUMMER ENDED in a cold snap, and Priscilla was so busy nursing her garden, she paid little attention to the Bradys. Her interest revived a little when Mr. Brady unloaded sacks of manure from his car and lugged them into the backyard. But whatever planting was going on, he asked no advice from Priscilla.

As fall deepened into winter, Priscilla saw even less of the Bradys. At Halloween, they did not hand out candy to neighborhood children. At Christmas, when the street was gay with outdoor lights, their house was dark. Early one January morning, a moving van pulled up in front of the Brady house. When Priscilla got home from work, she found boxes of trash on the curb. Next door, the curtainless front windows had the blank look of an empty house.

By the gate to the stockade fence, stood Marty Kovack, a familiar scowling figure. When Priscilla was growing up, Marty was the boy next door. They had dated for a while, but he had married someone else. For years he had rented out his old family home, along with a dozen other properties he owned. Now he was trying to sell.

"Would you believe it," Marty called to her as he walked over. "Those Bradys backed out of the lease purchase, and I'm stuck with this house again."

"Why did they leave?" Priscilla asked.

"I only talked to the husband," Marty said. "His wife didn't like the area, and he couldn't make enough money. They moved to Seattle. Well, they lost out on a nice little house, that's all I can say. Why don't you buy it, Prissy? It would be a good investment."

"One house is all I can handle, Marty," she replied.

"Can't say I blame you," he said. "There's money in real estate but a lot of headaches, too. I should know."

"I'm sure you'll find a buyer," Priscilla murmured.

"Not with what I found in the back yard," Marty said. "Hey, maybe you can help me out. You like to plant flowers. Take a look at this."

Priscilla followed Marty through the gate and caught her breath in awe. In a corner of the yard was a steaming compost pile twice as large as her own. How had Mr. Brady managed it? She fussed and fussed with her own compost, but could never heat it to steaming hot.

"How am I going to sell this house with that thing in the back yard," Marty complained. "It looks like a volcano."

"It's a compost pile, Marty, the best fertilizer in the world. Rake it over the yard, and you'll have a beautiful lawn this summer."

"If you say so, Prissy. But my back can't take that kind of work no more."

Priscilla thought fast. With all that compost she could put in a vegetable patch. The seed catalogs had begun to come in the mail, and, for some reason, eggplant had caught her attention.

"If you give me a week or two, I can take care of it," she offered. "I'll take a few wheelbarrow loads for my garden and spread the rest."

"How much are you gonna take?" he asked. "You said this stuff is good for my grass."

"I'll leave plenty for your grass, Marty. Is it a deal?"

"It's a deal. You always were a big help to me, Prissy. We go back a long way, you know."

Priscilla knew what was coming next and brought out her usual defense.

"How's your family, Marty?" she asked.

A BAD cold and an out-of-town conference kept Priscilla from the compost pile in Marty's yard until Valentine's Day. By then it no longer steamed triumphantly, but looked gray and cold.

What a lot of work he put into his pile, Priscilla thought, probably to escape his awful wife. Poor man, she hoped composting had brought him some happiness.

By afternoon Priscilla's back and arms throbbed, but she had transferred half of the compost to a new raised bed and had raked the rest over Marty's yard. The glorious black soil, marred only by a few scattered bones, had a faintly unpleasant odor. Leaning on her shovel and dreaming of spring, Priscilla noticed something gleaming in the dark soil.

You find the strangest things in compost, she thought, as she pulled out a small gold ring. Priscilla wondered uneasily if Mrs. Brady had lost her wedding ring in the compost. She would have to get her address from Marty and return it. On closer inspection, she recognized the ring for what it was – a toe ring. The girls at the bank wore them all the time. Real gold from the look of it, and not cheap, not with that engraved leaf pattern. It must have come off as Mrs. Brady walked barefoot in the grass. No doubt she was sorry to lose it, but a toe ring didn't have the sentimental value of a wedding band. There was no reason to take the trouble of returning it. Priscilla put the ring in her pocket and went back to dreaming about summer vegetable gardens.

She stirred the compost with the tip of her shovel. A faint breeze wafted the unpleasant odor to her nostrils, as though trying to draw her attention. Looking more closely at the scattered bones, she recalled the poster of a spine on the wall of her chiropractor's office – odd that the bones in the compost looked like human vertebrae. She felt for the toe ring in her pocket. Little Mrs. Brady was barely half the size of the sow composted at the Ag College. Was it possible? Priscilla shook her head in angry denial to clear the sudden, unwelcome vision of policemen raking through her raised beds and digging up Marty's lawn. Stop imagining things, she ordered herself. Somewhere on the West Coast, Mr. Brady still tried to please his demanding wife as they lived out their miserable married life.

Next summer, the compost would produce a bumper crop of eggplant. She would share them with all her neighbors, maybe even give Marty a few. And, she would wear the toe ring herself. She wasn't too old, despite what Mrs. Brady had said.

She should be grateful that Mrs. Brady lost her ring. What a pity she couldn't thank her in person.

DEAD MAN'S TREASURE

KB INGLEE

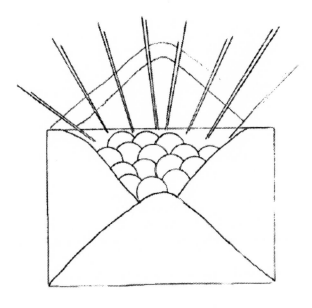

The hammering at her kitchen door so startled Charlotte Wyngate that she lost her grip on the flowered teacup and spilled hot tea on the back of her hand. She was alone in the building and was expecting no one.

The proper entrance to Miss Wyngate's apartment was from the third floor of the school, next to the chemistry lab. But she had a private entrance that led from a locked door at street level to her kitchen. Only her cleaning lady and Virginia Pomeroy, her bosom friend, had keys to the door at the bottom.

"Who's there?" she called out cautiously, setting the cup down and drying her hand on a dishtowel.

"Joey. Dr. Pomeroy sent me to fetch you."

She opened the door to the street urchin who fetched and carried for Dr. Pomeroy's Women's Clinic.

"Mr. Vickers was stabbed just outside the clinic. She sent me for the cops then for you. You come right away."

"Did you go to the police?" she asked in her stern schoolteacher's voice, trying to remember who Vickers was. She had an image of a tall elderly man with a long stringy gray beard.

Joey nodded and handed her the key Dr. Pomeroy had entrusted to him. They stood staring at each other for several heartbeats, she the tall, lean, aging headmistress of The Cambridge School for Girls, and he, the ragged, self-assured, ten-year old boy inadequately dressed for the chilly winter evening.

"Wait here while I get my coat and hat," she said breaking the silence.

When she returned to the kitchen, the cake on the sideboard was one slice smaller and Joey was licking the remnants of chocolate icing off his fingers, looking triumphantly guilty.

"We'd best bustle," she said, pretending not to notice the cake theft. "It's already dark."

The mismatched pair hurried down Orange Street toward the river.

"What happened? Is he dead? Was he murdered? Is Dr. Pomeroy all right? Was anyone else hurt?"

"Dr. Pomeroy sent me out to get the scissors she took to be sharpened this morning. When I got back Mr. Vickers was all in a heap on the front stoop."

"He was dead?" she repeated.

"He died after we got him inside and into a bed. Dr. Pomeroy stopped the blood, and did some other stuff, but he died anyhow."

"Who did it?"

"Don't know. I didn't see nobody but him."

"Did he say anything?"

"He said this would cure him of talking too much."

"Do you have any idea what he meant by that?"

Joey shook his head with such vigor that Miss Wyngate knew he was hiding something.

After a short silence Joey went on, "I liked him. He had me find things for him. He would give me a penny if I found just what he was looking for."

"What kinds of things?" she asked.

"Bits of metal, pipe, scraps of leather. He asked for an egg beater once."

"My father, he is an inventor, you know, used to get my brother and me to find things like that for him. I gave him my mother's eggbeater. She was furious, but I was a penny richer." This was hardly the kind of tale she should be telling a lad with such uncertain morals.

"You have to tell the police what you know, Joey," she advised, wondering if it would do any good to appeal to his conscience or the greater good. If he wouldn't tell her or Dr. Pomeroy what he knew, he would never tell the police. She would have to find out and tell them herself.

Their progress was slowed at every intersection by carriages headed for the evening entertainment at the Grand Opera House. At this late hour, the commercial traffic on Front Street was lighter. At Tatnall Street they turned toward the river, crossed the railroad tracks and entered the refurbished factory building that was now Dr. Pomeroy's clinic.

In the dim light, Miss Wyngate saw the screen drawn around the bed in the far corner. A nurse looked up from her task with one of the three patients, and nodded as they came in.

Behind the back wall of the ward were offices, dispensary and a room that was half kitchen half staff parlor. Virginia Pomeroy could be seen through what had once been the paymaster's window.

"Oh, Lottie, you've come. Where are the police?"

"Virginia, what happened?" asked Miss Wyngate, hurrying to her friend.

Though Dr. Pomeroy was a few years younger and several inches shorter than Miss Wyngate, she had a few pounds on her. Miss Wyngate had always thought Dr. Pomeroy looked substantial and elegant in her black frock coat and gray skirt that mimicked the dress of male doctors. Now she simply looked old.

"Joey found Vickers in the street outside the clinic," said Dr. Pomeroy, sounding tired. "We brought him in, and he died here. I tried to save him, Lottie."

"Miss Wyngate, what are you doing here?" asked the policeman standing at the office door. She hadn't heard him come into the room.

"Sergeant McDermott," Miss Wyngate said, introducing the man she had met in equally distressing circumstances several months earlier, "this is Dr. Virginia Pomeroy. The man in the bed behind the screen was murdered outside the clinic this evening. Dr. Pomeroy tried to save him."

"She calls her friend before she alerts the police?" asked McDermott, as he helped Miss Wyngate out of her coat. Though a maiden lady well past marriageable age, Charlotte Wyngate was not beyond appreciating a good-looking man when she ran into one. McDermott was tall with dark twinkling eyes and a handlebar mustache of which he was justly proud.

"No, sir," Joey cut in, alternately diffident and defiant. "I went to the police first, then to get Miss Wyngate, just like Dr. Pomeroy said."

Miss Wyngate nodded.

"He was alive when you brought him in?" asked the Sergeant.

Dr. Pomeroy stared at the policeman, but did not speak. Miss Wyngate dropped her hand tenderly onto her friend's shoulder.

"What did he die of?" asked the policeman.

In her distress Dr. Pomeroy took refuge in what she understood best, science.

"He was stabbed. It was a thin blade, about ten inches long, half an inch wide, and very sharp. It entered the left side under the ribs and up. The man who did it is right handed, your height or a bit shorter, Sergeant. He is very skilled in the use of that knife." Dr. Pomeroy's voice was barely audible. Her eyes dropped from the sergeant's face to her hands folded on the desk in front of her.

"How do you know all that?" asked Miss Wyngate, amazed, as she always was at her friend's powers of observation.

"When you have worked with these women for as long as I have, you come to know the abusers almost as well as you know the victims," Dr. Pomeroy admitted.

"Do you have the knife?" asked McDermott.

Dr. Pomeroy shook her head.

"Do you know who the victim is?" he asked.

"Yes," Dr. Pomeroy answered softly. "John Vickers. He worked here from time to time, fixing things."

"He keep regular hours? Come every day?"

"No, just when he needed some extra money."

"Where did he live?" Sergeant McDermott was polite but persistent.

"On one of those streets the other side of Harlan and Hollingsworth, near the dry docks. I don't know the name, if it even has one. Joey, here, can tell you where it is."

"Any family?"

Dr. Pomeroy shrugged and remained silent. Miss Wyngate took a key out of the top drawer of the desk, unlocked the medicine cabinet and removed a dark brown bottle from the rear of the top shelf. She poured two fingers' worth of amber liquid into a dose glass and handed it to Dr. Pomeroy.

"Medicinal brandy," explained Miss Wyngate to the policeman as she relocked the bottle in the cabinet and returned the key to the desk drawer.

After taking a small sip of the brandy, Dr. Pomeroy described Mr. Vickers' death. "He left here at three seventeen this afternoon. Probably went to drink at his usual place over by the iron works. He might walk by the clinic to get home if he went along the river. We brought him in at five forty seven. It was getting dark. He was unable to speak, and lost consciousness almost at once. He died at six-o-two."

"Ever been to his house, ma'am?"

Dr. Pomeroy shook her head again. Sergeant McDermott waited quietly for her to go on. "He seemed to have enough money to live on. What he made here was only enough to pay for a drink or two. Good whiskey seemed to be his only real luxury."

"Show me, if you would," McDermott requested, inclining his head toward the screen in the corner of the ward.

Miss Wyngate watched through the window as Dr. Pomeroy took the Sergeant to view the body.

Joey tugged at her sleeve. "Miss Wyngate?

"Humm?"

"Is Dr. Pomeroy all right?"

"No, Joey, she isn't. She has dedicated her life to healing. Her friend was stabbed on her doorstep, and she was unable to save him."

"I never seen her like this before. Not even when Ma died."

"Your mother died here?"

"Yes, ma'am. My Pa, he's OK. Works for the ferry to Philadelphia. He ain't home a lot. Sometimes I stay here, sometimes I stay with Mr. Vickers."

"If you won't tell the police what you know, you must tell me or Dr. Pomeroy," Miss Wyngate told the boy.

He thought for a bit before answering.

"Maybe whoever killed him wanted his treasure." Joey closed his mouth so firmly that Miss Wyngate thought he might never speak again. She waited. "He told me not to tell anybody. I never did 'til now, but he talked about it sometimes. Nobody from Wilmington believed he was rich. Sometimes if they was from somewhere else, they thought it was real. He always said his treasure might not be someone else's treasure. But treasures are always jewels or gold or something, aren't they?"

"Not always. Do you have something you would never part with, no matter what happened?"

Joey reached into his pocket and pulled out his hand closed into a tight fist. He opened his hand a finger at a time revealing a piece of blue beach glass.

"Ma had it on the window in our kitchen. I took it after she died and Pa moved us into a room down by the ferry dock."

"Then that is your treasure. If I were to take it from you, your heart would be broken, but it would have no value for me."

His eyes told her he understood. She closed his hand around the shard and smiled at him. "Dr. Pomeroy will be all right in a day or two."

"You'll be here later, Dr. Pomeroy?" asked McDermott as they came back into the office. "I gotta make my report, and send the police doctor along to take a look at the body. We'll be at this for some time, but I imagine we can leave some of it 'til morning."

"I have a telephone, Sergeant, if that will help." Dr. Pomeroy pointed to a cabinet on the wall by the door to the ward.

"If you got a telephone, why didn't you call the police, rather than send a boy along?" asked the Sergeant with the slightest tone of accusation in his voice.

Dr. Pomeroy looked bewildered by the question. "Miss Wyngate doesn't answer the phone in the evening," Dr. Pomeroy offered as a none too coherent excuse.

Miss Wyngate was surprised that the police didn't know about the clinic's phone, since they often stopped by the school to use hers. Maybe a building full of sick women was less appealing than a building full of healthy girls.

"The doctor will be along soon," McDermott reported when he hung up.

Dr. Pomeroy requested in a quiet but firm voice, "Please, can we keep the uproar at a minimum? I may have only three patients, but they do need their rest."

Dr. Pomeroy's plea came just as two patrolmen joined McDermott.

Dr. Ticknor wasn't far behind. He smiled at the women through his full red beard, and patted Dr. Pomeroy on the arm. Both women were pleased to see their friend had come in place of the regular police surgeon.

IT WAS nearly ten o'clock when Dr. Ticknor finished and sent the body off on the police cart to the mortuary.

"I'm sorry you are involved in this, Dr. Pomeroy," he said, his accent so slight that neither woman had been able to identify it in all the years they had known him. "I am not a policeman, but it does not look like you will be a suspect. Must have been a drunken brawl."

"Why, then," asked Dr. Pomeroy reasonably, "is his only wound the hole in him? No bruising on his knuckles or face, so he neither delivered nor received a blow. His clothes were not in disarray. Does that make me a suspect again?"

"Your observations may be correct, but I hardly think you could have done it. Surely your nurse and your patients will vouch for you," he said thoughtfully. Then, turning to Miss Wyngate, he offered, "Let me take you home. You should not be walking the streets at this hour. If I know the charming Dr. Pomeroy, she will spend the night right here." He gestured toward the closed door of the next room where he knew there was a cot for just such emergencies.

Miss Wyngate, after assuring herself that Dr. Pomeroy would be all right in the care of the night nurse, accepted gratefully.

Once they were rolling up Tatnall Street, Dr. Ticknor commented, "I do not much like the way Dr. Pomeroy is taking this. I have never known her to be so shaken."

"No," admitted Miss Wyngate, "it's not like her. She's used to violence and death. Even Joey commented on it."

"She is used to women who have been abused in one way or another. Murder is something quite different. The man was attacked on her doorstep and she failed to save him. We doctors take that sort of thing very seriously."

"I'll go back to the clinic in the morning. If she needs to be looked after, I'll see that she is."

Dr. Ticknor handed Miss Wyngate out of the carriage, and walked her to the stairs that lead to her kitchen. He took the key from her hand and unlocked the door. Returning the key firmly to her grasp, he said, "Call me tomorrow, lest I worry overmuch about her. She is my friend, too."

Miss Wyngate wanted to kiss the funny little man, but she restrained herself, shook his hand, thanked him and fled up the stairs to her sanctuary.

SHE HAD planned to spend Saturday editing the article she and Mr. Carlisle, the science teacher, were writing for "The Journal of New Education." It was already overdue, and though the editor had forgiven them one deadline, he would not forgive another.

Remembering her promise to Dr. Ticknor, and her own concern for her friend, she headed for the clinic, instead.

When Miss Wyngate arrived, Dr. Pomeroy was sitting on the edge of one of the beds talking to the patients. The screen was gone from the corner and the bed was remade and spotless. The signs of death were always removed quickly so as not to disturb the living. Two women in gray dresses and white aprons bustled about the ward as though it were any ordinary day. Joey, who had still been at the clinic when Miss Wyngate left, was feeding logs to the stove.

"I suppose the police will be back soon," said Dr. Pomeroy with a sigh, leaving her patients and coming to greet her friend. "Why are you here?"

Not wanting to let Dr. Pomeroy know how worried she was, Miss Wyngate said, "I have some experience with the police. I might be of help to you."

"I haven't done a bit of medicine this morning." Dr. Pomeroy looked discouraged, but not as withdrawn as she had been last evening. "The police visit has been better tonic than anything in my cabinets. My patients want to hear about what happened to Mr. Vickers. If they are well enough to gossip they are well enough to go home."

"Did you get any sleep last night?" asked Miss Wyngate, already knowing the answer.

Dr. Pomeroy's shoulders sagged. "Very little. I'm exhausted. I can put up a good front with my patients, but I've never been able to hide anything from you. I'm glad you came."

"You seem to know a good deal about a handyman," commented Miss Wyngate.

"A woman's clinic is a hotbed of gossip, and I found out a lot about him from my patients. He drinks with one husband, works for another. Besides we shared tea from time to time when it was quiet here. He was not talkative, but he said enough. He was well read and loved literature though he had little formal education. We were friends of sorts."

"And Sergeant McDermott isn't so bad looking, either," teased Miss Wyngate, hoping to bring a little color back into her friend's tired face. "I expect we will get one of the Captains this morning, maybe a matron as well, since this is a women's clinic. You shouldn't be chatting with your patients until the police have questioned them."

"They did, last night after you left. No one knew a thing except my bringing Mr. Vickers in and staying with him. They did tell the police that I hadn't left the clinic after Mr. Vickers died, though."

"Good, at least I won't have to visit you in jail."

A variety of expressions crossed Dr. Pomeroy's face, as though she were uncertain how to take such a remark from her friend, wanting to pass it off as humor, and afraid to take it seriously. At length her eyes wandered to the painting on the wall, a poorly executed watercolor of the clinic with the Christina River, brown and sluggish, in the background.

CAPTAIN THOMAS Kane, a tall bony man with dark hair, arrived at the clinic as Dr. Pomeroy was preparing tea.

"Good morning, ladies." He nodded politely to the doctor and the teacher. "Just got back from Vickers' place. It was in a shambles, like someone had just thrown everything around. I must admit I always thought the man was a vagrant, but it seems he owned his place, humble as it was."

Dr. Pomeroy offered what she knew of the man in a weary voice. "He wasn't a pauper so much as an ascetic. He told me once that his belongings fit into two categories, those that nourished the body and those that nourished the soul. He drank, but he wasn't a drunkard. When he left here in the evening, he would spend what he made, but never more. He would get tipsy, but never falling down drunk. He didn't make enough, and he liked high quality whisky. He said all he needed were his liquor and his letters. He seemed to have everything he needed. He was never hungry when he came here; not like some of the others."

"Joey must be right; they were looking for his treasure," commented Miss Wyngate.

"What treasure?" asked Dr. Pomeroy showing her first spark of real interest.

"Apparently he used to brag about some treasure of his. He did qualify his brag by saying what was treasure for him might not be treasure for another. Joey told me that his last words were something about learning not to talk so much. He could have meant that his bragging caught the wrong person's attention."

"That would explain why someone tore his place apart. I must admit, we didn't find much either," mused the policeman.

"We did find this, though." Captain Kane handed Dr. Pomeroy an envelope. "Seems to be a will of sorts. It mentions a treasure, but doesn't specify. After taking a look at his place, we thought it was a joke, or something only the two of you would understand."

The envelope bore Dr. Pomeroy's name in the flowing hand of a professional scrivener. Inside was a document in identical hand. She read it out loud. Mr. Vickers, having no family, had left all his goods and chattels to the clinic with the exception of "My treasure, which I leave personally to Dr. Virginia Pomeroy, to do with as she pleases."

"All you have to do is find it," said Kane, clearly not believing a word that Vickers had written. "We'll let you know when we're done with the house if you want to go look for this treasure no one else has been able to find."

McDermott glanced through the windows into the ward. "Where's the young man who found Vickers?"

Dr. Pomeroy opened the door into the staff room to reveal the lad in question curled up on the cot sound asleep.

"He was up most of the night. I think he was trying to take care of me."

"We'll question him later." Captain Kane laughed, bowed formally and was gone.

"This has been difficult for you," said Miss Wyngate. "How about a hot meal at the Clayton House? I have some change rattling around in the bottom of my purse."

"I wouldn't mind having someone else cook and clean up. Something hot would be just what the doctor ordered." Dr. Pomeroy took a dollar bill out of a lock box in her desk drawer. "I think the clinic owes us that much. If the board objects, I'll have Dr. Ticknor write us a prescription for it."

Both women had underestimated the speed with which news spread through Wilmington. Instead of a private meal, they spent the hour explaining the details to every waiter, the desk clerk and the owner himself.

"Dr. Pomeroy, Miss Wyngate," Sergeant McDermott called to them from the steps of the City Hall as they left the hotel.

They stood where they were, uncomfortably aware of the number of people who were staring at them.

"Ah, I was on my way to let you know we arrested a Mr. Josiah Watson for the murder of your Mr. Vickers. Vickers had been bragging about his treasure, and Watson, from someplace down-river, had overheard him. Most people who drank regularly with Vickers knew the treasure was all in his mind, but this Watson took it seriously. It wasn't even dark when Vickers left the saloon and Watson just stuck him and left him in the street, then went and tore his place apart looking for gold. Lucky for Vickers it was outside your place, so he could die among friends. Here's the key. You can go hunt for your treasure now if you want."

"Yes, lucky," said Dr. Pomeroy vaguely, staring at the key, but not taking it.

"Are you sure he did it, Sergeant?" asked Miss Wyngate, knowing from experience they didn't always arrest the right man.

"Yes, ma'am. He had a knife on him like the one Dr. Ticknor said to look for. Fit the description he gave, too. He admitted it when we found the weapon."

Both women, used to having their own hard work and knowledge attributed to men ignored the reference to Dr. Ticknor.

"Let's go take a look, shall we?" asked Miss Wyngate taking the offered key.

THOUGH THE contents of Vickers' one room house had been strewn about, the basic order was still visible under the wreckage. He had been neat and tidy, a trait that made him invaluable to the clinic. The room was clearly divided into sections, for sleeping, working, and cooking.

Morning sun would fall across the bed through the small southeastern windows. The work area was lit, now, by the afternoon sun pouring through two larger windows facing southwest. There was plenty of light for detailed work at the table that filled the corner next to the fireplace. The kitchen along the north wall consisted of a sink with a single tap, small coal range, and a piece of furniture that was part table, part pantry. An oil lamp lay shattered in the sink.

Clothing, bed linen, kitchen utensils, and tools from the workbench had been thrown into a heap in the center of the room.

In the work area Miss Wyngate began to smooth out the crumpled, torn and discarded papers. They contained a series of schematic diagrams for items that made no sense to her. She caressed one of the drawings lovingly and smiled.

Dr. Pomeroy was looking at a small open stove that had been pulled halfway out of the fireplace. "What's this?" she asked.

"It's a forge. There's the anvil, over there. Watson must have tried the bricks behind it looking for a hiding place."

Picking up a shard of the blown glass globe used to focus lamplight on a small area, she added, "Mr. Vickers was an inventor, like my father. I expect he made a living making one-of-a-kind items for the factories around here."

"An inventor like your father?" Dr. Pomeroy echoed. "He made several things for the clinic, most were quite crude, but they worked well and came in handy when we couldn't afford the real thing from a medical supply house in Philadelphia. One probe was exquisite in its simplicity."

"Joey told me Vickers paid him to find scrap, just as my father paid Robert and me when we were children." Miss Wyngate turned away from the workbench that was so familiar to her, and took in the rest of the room.

One single area stood out in the chaos. A shelf above the bed, with some books and a bundle of letters, had not been disturbed.

"Why do you think he would overlook the bookshelf?" asked Dr. Pomeroy following Miss Wyngate's gaze.

"Perhaps he thought it too small to hold any significant treasure. Or maybe he's illiterate, so even if this were the treasure, he would have no way of knowing."

Miss Wyngate pulled down one of the books. Longfellow Poems, "Paul Revere's Ride," "The Village Blacksmith," and several others. She set it back and retrieved a copy of *The Scarlet Letter*. Both books were well worn, and inscribed with the name Thomas Garrett, as were the other books on the shelf.

Miss Wyngate handed *The Legend of Sleepy Hollow* to her friend, open to show the inscription in the front. The faded ink read, "To John Vickers, in appreciation, Tho Garrett."

"Mr. Vickers was always very proud of having worked for Thomas Garrett. I guess that would have been something to be proud of, once."

"Who's Thomas Garrett?" asked Miss Wyngate. "The name is familiar, but I can't place it. There's a Francis Garrett on the board of my church, perhaps some relative?"

Dr. Pomeroy stared at her friend wide-eyed.

"You've lived in Wilmington for over ten years and you don't know who Thomas Garrett was? You pride yourself on being from an old New England abolitionist family and you don't know who Thomas Garrett was? You know Francis Garrett, and you never asked him about his famous relative?"

Miss Wyngate shook her head, more interested than repentant.

"He was a Wilmington Quaker of some worth who lost everything providing a safe passage for escaping slaves. He's dead now."

"The Underground Railroad," mused Miss Wyngate.

"That seems like such a long time ago," Dr. Pomeroy went on, "but when I was a child, I can remember my parents talking about how brave Garrett was. Not many people, though they took chances, were willing to forfeit their fortune for their conscience. Usually people seem to preserve both."

Miss Wyngate picked up the bundle of letters and untied the once red ribbon that bound it. The first was addressed to Garrett, and was dated Concord, Massachusetts, 1852. The signature, like the rest of the writing was faded and nearly illegible.

She carried it to the window and tipped the paper so that it caught every scrap of light.

"Oh, my," she sighed, refolded the letter reverently and took another. "They're all the same," she said reading signature after signature. "This is part of a correspondence between Thomas Garrett and Bronson Alcott."

"Bronson Alcott? Who's that?" asked Dr. Pomeroy with a mocking half smile on her face.

"Virginia, I'm shocked," said Miss Wyngate, with a wry smile. "With you being so well read, especially Emerson and the other Concord transcendentalists."

"The name is familiar, but I can't place it," admitted Dr. Pomeroy in Miss Wyngate's own words.

"Of course it is. He was Louisa May Alcott's father, well known in his own right as a philosopher and educator. I use many of his methods myself. He worked for a time at a school in Germantown. He must have met Garrett then. The letters are dated after the Alcotts moved back to Massachusetts."

"This is the treasure, isn't it?" asked Dr. Pomeroy, gently caressing a volume she held.

Miss Wyngate smiled, knowing she had to be right. "Not if you think of value in dollars. It probably isn't worth anything. But we all have a different idea of what a treasure is. For me it's my library, for you it is your reputation among the poor women of Wilmington."

"Or our friendship," added Dr. Pomeroy, setting down the book and taking Miss Wyngate's hand.

LES FLEURS DEMENTOS

JUSTYNN TYME

Arthur came home as usual from the meat packaging plant; he hated that place with a passion. He was undercover, a spy for an animal rights organization, sent in to watch and learn. But he had been there so long he was sure they had forgotten about him. Arthur sent his weekly emails and his monthly pictures, and all he ever got back was a thank you note with a p.s. about keeping up the good work. At least it was something, but it hardly sufficed; he was sick to death of this place. Arthur was loyal, always sticking it out, even though every day he entertained numerous day dreams about not only quitting, but jumping on that conveyer belt and letting himself get chopped up and sent off to some unsuspecting grocery store just so he wouldn't have to live with the memories anymore.

He knew a pig once, Suzy. He was proud to call her friend, but here he was butchering her friends, cousins, brothers or sisters. Maybe even Suzy had gone zipping down the butcher line, and he would have never known. Then he heard it, another truck full of innocent pink piggies, victims of a capitalistic death sentence. For Arthur this was the last straw. No more. He couldn't do it anymore. He took off his shoes and socks, climbed onto the belt and lay down. This was it; he was going to do it. He was going to end it all. Arthur was smiling as he went rumbling down the line. Waving at all the poor saps that had no idea how truly horrible their jobs really were. As he jostled along down the line, he just sort of watched himself riding along.

Suddenly, he was jarred awake. Mike Collaza, his boss, was hulking over him. So close in fact, that Arthur could feel Mike's eyelashes brush against his face when he blinked. Mike was yelling at him something awful this time. He was storming on and on about Arthur's constant day dreaming. Mike emphasized the point by slapping his hand on the thin rubber belt of the conveyor, which chimed like a cheap tambourine. He rehashed the fact that Arthur could lose a finger, an arm, or even his life if he wasn't paying attention. More importantly, he'd lose his job. Then Mike puffed up for one hell of a bellow and let fly one last thing.

"Now get back to work! Get them porkers popping down the line, damn it!" He said it so the entire plant, even above the incessant whining of the machinery, could hear him. Arthur, a bit rattled, waited for the next piggy to come thumping down the shoot. He heard the thump, but what came out of the shoot wasn't a pig. It was a big bundle of colorful flowers. Half perplexed, he didn't know what do with them, so he pulled them off the line and threw them to the side behind him. Then, thump,

thump, out of the shoot came another bundle of flowers, and then another and another and another. It was like a scene out of the "I Love Lucy Show." His co-workers were all staring blankly, at him, at the flowers, but not saying a word.

Mike came back around to check on Arthur and saw the pile of flowers, and turned a rather flattering shade of red. With mustard calmness, saturated with sarcasm, he asked, "How long have you worked here, Arty?"

"Ah, about nine months," Arthur said feeling almost eight-years-old again.

"Since when do we throw the product on the floor?"

"Er... I haven't. I mean, they're supposed to be pigs coming down the line." He was conscious of everything shutting down around him. Everything becoming very, very quiet except for Mike's loud shirt and piercing glare.

"Pigs! Since when? This has been a green house for almost twenty years."

Arthur looked around at the high glass walls and the glass ceiling. He looked around at all the flowers, hundreds of different varieties. All tickling the eye with their brilliant colors.

"Where are all the chopping and slicing machines?" Arthur was in a daze now. He had no idea where he was or how he got there. He just stood there swaying under the awesome power of disbelief.

"Chopping and slicing machines!?! Look son..." Mike said quite sensitively "...there is something seriously wrong with you. Pick up that crap you threw on the floor and go home."

Arthur looked down and saw seven pigs lying on the floor. He looked back at Mike and Mike's head was a cluster of hyacinths and the blooms fluttered when he spoke. Arthur's eyes swelled up with fear; flowers were appearing and disappearing disconcertingly. Arthur never really liked flowers. He knew they knew that and they hated him all the more for it. They were fiddling with his brains just for fun.

ARTHUR RAN. He ran like a whirlwind. He blasted out of the building not wanting to look back, but something was tugging at his sub-consciousness, and he had to turn around. It was huge and towering above him like a B-rated movie monster. A giant bunch of poinsettias was looming over him. He shook his head again and again in disbelief, and when he was finally able to focus, it was gone. Nothing was there now except a vast landscape. His eyes slowly trailed down toward the ground, and there were the poinsettias nestled at his feet in a crudely painted clay pot. He looked up in fear hoping the poinsettias hadn't seen him looking, and his eyes nearly popped out of his head. He was surrounded. Tulips were everywhere as far as the eye could see. He screamed like a little girl and once again ran for his life, busting through the hordes of tulips like a rhino in a cracker factory, swinging and swiping as if his arms were machetes.

ARTHUR RAN blindly through the horrid field of tulips, fleeing from everywhere, escaping to nowhere. He began to cry. True he never liked flowers, but he never wanted them expunged off the face of the earth. Yet here they were playing mind games with him. Possibly, they were going to snuff him out just for spite. Then through his tears, out of the corner of his eye, he saw something. He swiveled his head around to get a better look, hoping it wasn't giant bellflowers ready to swallow him up. It wasn't. What Arthur saw made him stop in his tracks. Piggies, dozen and dozens of them, all leaping playfully like dolphins through the tulips. He could hear beautiful singing like angels. He began to run toward them, and they in turn began to move toward Arthur. He was smiling and they were smiling. He laughed and they squealed with delight. Arthur flung his arms open wide, ready to hug the first melodious pink piggie that came to him. Then his foot caught on a treacherous root, and, with a thud, he flopped face down onto the ground.

A FEW nurses came running into the featureless lounge to see a patient, his foot inexplicably stuck in his shin-high nightshirt, sprawled so comically in the middle of the floor they nearly laughed. The nurses merely chuckled as they hoisted him off the floor and back into a chair. Then one of the nurses noticed something that irked her.

"Who put this plant on the radiator again? Excessive heat isn't good for some plants. God knows what it does to them. Do not set this primrose on the radiator again, please!"

Street

Smarts

J. Gregory Smith

Baltimore, MD Johns Hopkins University, 2015

They called it *the Wolf.* Graduate student Gina Torreta knew the official name for the virus, but everyone, including Dr. Choy, referred to it by its nickname. Short for "the Wolf in sheep's clothing," which described the insidious way the virus worked.

Gina shivered and crossed Madison Street. She approached the entrance to the Broadway Research building, part of Johns Hopkins Medical School. She reached into her purse for her ID card, but spotted "Al" camped in a nook along the side of the building. He huddled in a discarded sleeping bag and scribbled on a flat piece of cardboard. His trademark wild gray hair made him immediately recognizable. She called him Al because she didn't know his real name, and he looked like Einstein on a bad hair day.

She tended to ignore the homeless around her in Baltimore. Her work with a world-renowned doctor in the field of genetic engineering and disease, made her wonder what she could do on a practical level. She wasn't a social worker; she was a scientist. Well, going to be, if she survived graduate school.

The first time she saw Al, there was something about him. Over the last few weeks she started to look out for him. She gave him food and some money, though he wasn't all that interested in cash. He was strange, but Gina never felt that he was "off" in a dangerous way. Neither did the security guards who tolerated him near the buildings. Sometimes the incoherent rants and raves of the homeless near the bus stop frightened her. She carried pepper spray for her walk from the bus to her tiny apartment.

Al was different. He had a warm, friendly expression and his eyes twinkled with humor and intelligence. He didn't speak much, but when he did she could only pick out a few words or phrases. She thought she could detect an accent, possibly German. She didn't speak more than a few phrases but had queried him with "Sprechen sie deutsche?" one morning. His eyes widened, but he didn't reply. Mostly he said "thank you" or "please" to passers-by.

Gina usually found him hard at work on his "manifesto," a long rambling tract written on a collection of flat cardboard he kept bundled in twine. Once she was able to read something about radio waves and government conspiracy. It was about what she expected. Her friends sometimes referred to him as the "nutty professor."

Whenever he was around, she tried to take a moment out of her overscheduled life to say hello or give him a snack. When the weather started to turn colder she brought him a sweater she'd picked up from a thrift shop. The look of gratitude and recognition in his eyes warmed her heart.

"Morning, Al. You doing okay, today?" He looked up from his writing and smiled before he finished his thought. His dirty hand clutched a worn pencil that looked like he sharpened it on the sidewalk.

"You got the cure for cancer there? Let us know when you have it knocked, huh?" Al looked at her sharply for an instant then smiled again. She pulled a candy bar and a banana out of her purse.

"Okay Al, I brought too much for lunch, which one do you want?"

He looked up and shrugged, as if to say: *Whatever you want, I just work here.*

"Okay, you can have the candy bar. I missed my workout yesterday, so the banana is enough."

He took the bar and tucked it into the sleeping bag.

"Alright, I'm off to try and save humanity. If you figure it out first, tell the guard to buzz me, okay?"

He nodded and gave a little wave.

For some reason, Al always made Gina feel better. Too often, homeless people made her feel sad (when they didn't frighten her) but Al was different.

She was grateful for the opportunity to work for a scientist of Dr. Choy's caliber and more than a little frightened by what they were up against.

Dr. Choy was part of the original team tasked to identify the virus later designated as *the Wolf* when he had been with the Center for Disease Control in Atlanta. Once the team created a reliable way of identifying the virus, the next step was to develop a vaccine against it and a cure for those who contracted it.

Years later the problems associated with *the Wolf* spread, and the Government turned to the private sector. Dr. Choy took the opportunity to join Johns Hopkins to continue his research.

Gina remembered Dr. Choy's lecture to an audience of laypersons and reporters on what was known about *the Wolf* to try and lend a sense of perspective to the disease. Currently, it was 100% lethal to those who contracted it. When it had first started to gain notoriety *the Wolf* was about as communicable as AIDS, mostly through bodily fluid contact, but lately there had been some disturbing trends in Africa that indicated *the Wolf* was changing again.

Gina flipped through her scrapbook of articles that tracked the history of the disease. The headlines flashed by and painted a grim picture.

Wolf an Escaped Bioweapon?
Assassin Germ Turns on It's Creators
Wolf A Smart Germ: Hides in Body, Attacks Immune System Then Turns Flu Like
Blood Test for Wolf Approved But No Cure in Sight
Wolf First Deployed in Africa Scientists Suspect

There were many others but they tracked a similar theme. What started as a discrete weapon was out of control and continued to adapt.

Dr. Choy told Gina that one of the reasons the CDC was able to develop the test for the virus was because they had some of the notes from one of the original designers. The scientists were all dead, except one. The last one seen alive was the primary architect, a genius named Wolfgang Kruger. Kruger had been from the old East Germany. Shortly after the first notable outbreak of the disease, even before anyone in the public ever heard of *the Wolf*, he vanished without a trace.

The virus was mapped but Dr. Choy's team was no closer to a cure. When a victim contracted *the Wolf*, by the time he showed symptoms there was little they could do other than confirm what had killed him.

Under lab conditions, samples of the virus were subjected to antibiotics, infusions of white blood cells, and various chemical attacks. Incredibly, *the Wolf* sensed a host fighting back and disguised itself again until it could multiply in sufficient numbers to overwhelm the new threat. Only strong chemical attacks, or radiation were effective (including UV, which meant sunlight would at least keep the disease contained if a body were exposed to the elements). Of course, the host would be long dead before the virus died.

If detected, doctors found that large infusions of white blood cells could force *the Wolf* into hiding, but only until it gathered more strength. Realistically, even this limited effort was difficult to put into practice, especially in most African countries.

The CDC and World Health Organization expressed a collective sense of hope that many of the prevention and containment efforts that evolved during the battle against HIV and AIDS could be used for *the Wolf*. This held true for a number of years, and the pace to find a cure slackened. The CDC and U.S. Government decided to expand the efforts to the private sector, especially prominent research Universities.

Gina walked down the hall and took the stairs to the basement complex where she worked with Dr. Choy. As she buzzed herself in, Dr. Choy rushed out of his office. The bottom of his white lab coat flapped behind him. Something was wrong.

"Gina! Conference room, five minutes!"

He rarely showed such emotion.

"What's happening?"

"You see, you see." She only saw his back. He moved fast for such a short man.

Gina hurried to her office and picked up her notebook.

IN THE videoconference room Gina saw Dr. Hollings, a tenured biologist, and Dr. Whitman, an MD and specialist in disease, already waiting. The video screen showed several men in similar white coats. The leader of the Atlanta team, Dr. Singer, a haggard looking older man, appeared on the screen.

"Now that you're all here, I'll get right to the point. I'm sending over the latest data on what we've uncovered, including the gene maps and the test results. I'll give you the *Reader's Digest* version," Dr. Singer said. Dr. Choy looked at Gina in puzzlement at the reference as Singer continued.

"Recently in the Congo, we've been getting indications about an increase in *Wolf* cases. You've seen those reports." Singer paused. "Gentleman, it appears that we are now seeing airborne versions of the virus." There was a collective murmur. Singer broke in.

"Our gene maps show some subtle changes in the structure of the virus. We left some tissue exposed to air and UV down in our level five lab to see what would happen."

"You find?" Choy asked.

"*The Wolf* can't last outside the body forever, but the sample we just tested survived for nearly three days." Singer paused.

"Five times longer than before!" Hollings said.

"Correct. The virus has shown it can adapt to live outside the body. Now we're in a race against time. The WHO has a crash quarantine program, but we have to worry about a panic. More resources will be available, and we're briefing the Administration in a couple of hours." The video camera reproduced the concern on his face.

"We'll stay in touch, and send the coffee bill to Atlanta, okay?" Dr. Hollings said. His pallor betrayed his light tone, but Singer smiled before he broke the connection.

THE NEXT few weeks were mostly a blur for Gina and the team. They churned data at a furious pace, but in the end they had to admit little progress. To date, the WHO, working with the government of the Congo managed to keep the outbreak contained, mostly because the incidents occurred in a remote region. If the airborne *Wolf* broke into a large population the estimates were catastrophic.

Gina began to despair that the WHO and the world governments were going to conclude that the virus was unstoppable and would destroy all people who were found to be in infected areas. She knew governments weren't immune to panic either.

Dr. Choy developed a breakthrough in testing that could detect the virus in the air. His innovation supported the frontline health workers setting up potential quarantine zones. Even so, the mood around the lab became grimmer by the day. Even Dr. Choy began to look dejected.

The days ran into each other (weekends were for the real world she was trying to protect) and Gina fell into a dreary pattern. The only joy in her life came from her interactions with Al, an odd constant in her life. He survived, despite the cold weather, in the same spot as always. The campus police left him alone, and Gina asked them to keep an eye on him while she was not around. Al refused any better accommodations, and the few times he was taken to a shelter during a cold snap, he returned, cardboard notes neatly organized and hair wilder than ever.

Gina brought him hot drinks and fell into an easy one-sided banter with him. She chatted with him about her work, secure in the knowledge her secrets were safe with him. She thought it was cute the way he listened so intently.

ONE NIGHT she stole out of the lab with some writing supplies to give Al as a surprise. He was on his usual spot and sat quietly in his sleeping bag.

He smiled at her approach and gestured for her to sit.

"Hi Al, what's shaking?" she smiled. "Not too busy, huh?"

Al gestured to his worn pencil, now a useless stub, and shrugged.

Gina was exhausted, and her eyes were ringed in dark circles. She put her notebook down next to her large canvas purse and sat wearily. Notebook? Uh oh. She just broke a major rule. She completely forgot to leave it in her office. She debated returning it but knew it might look odd. The guards were nice, but they still had to log her in. Better to take it back in the morning.

"Have I got a surprise for you!" Gina reached into her bag and pulled out a box of pencils along with a sharpener. She had also filched a set of markers in various colors and a legal pad. His reaction refreshed her spirit.

Al crowed with delight as he took the pencils and markers. He studied each color before he placed it carefully back in the holder. He grinned at the pencil sharpener and nodded to Gina as if they had just shared the secrets of the ages. He put all the writing tools into his sleeping bag and glanced around furtively.

"Don't worry Al, nobody is going to take them from you."

He gave her a look that said: *If you only knew.*

She pushed the pad of paper toward him. He looked it over. To Gina's surprise, he placed the pad by her bag on top of her notebook. He picked up a blank square of cardboard and nodded, as if to say: *Thanks anyway, but I'll stick with this.*

Gina shrugged. "Okay, Al, you can keep working on that. Tell you what, I'll leave it just in case you change your mind. I have plenty of paper at work. No answers, but lots of space to put them on."

Gina felt the exhaustion wash over her body. She knew it was time to leave when Al's sleeping bag looked cozy. She grabbed her bag.

"Have a safe night, Al. I'll see you in the morning."

He smiled and waved. She trudged to the bus stop hoping she'd stay awake long enough to get off at the right stop.

When Gina got home, she barely remembered leaving the bus. She was asleep before her head hit the pillow.

THE NEXT morning she awoke with a vague sense of unease. She checked her alarm clock and saw she'd actually beat the buzzer by five minutes. She wasn't late, but something was definitely wrong. With a start, she looked over by her bag. Her notebook! Her heart leapt into her throat as she tried to reconstruct events to place where she last saw it. She struggled to clear her head. Her first thought was that she'd left it on the bus. So much of the ride home was a blank. Hell, so much of the last few weeks were a fog.

The notebook had no apparent monetary value, though in the wrong hands the story it told, among the scientific jargon and gene codes, could spark a panic.

Gina felt a panic of her own. The best-case scenario involved her termination for lax handling of classified materials. The thought brought her to tears. She sat on her worn couch and stared at the Monet print that brightened her otherwise spare apartment. After a few minutes, she gathered herself and walked through her bedroom to grab some tissue to blow her nose. On her bedroom wall was a framed version of an old picture of the real Albert Einstein, a classic shot of him sticking out his tongue. Some friends had given it to her as a kind of joke about her "boyfriend" on the streets.

The picture made her realize that the last time she could clearly recall her notebook was when she sat down last night to give Al his presents. Yes! She left that pad of paper and he put it over her notebook. If Al had her notebook she'd buy him a breakfast she couldn't afford for herself!

The bus crawled through the early morning traffic. Gina hopped off and resisted the urge to run. *Please, please, please let him have it*, she repeated through her head like a mantra.

She reached his spot and for a moment worried he wasn't there, but then the lump under the blankets and sleeping bag stirred.

"Al?"

A gray squirrel's nest poked out of the top of the blankets. Al's head emerged and his eyes focused on Gina. He crawled out from under the covers.

Gina forced herself to slow down. Even when fully awake, Al wasn't exactly in his right mind. He looked more worn out than usual.

Al stretched and grinned at her with a twinkle in his eyes. Gina always needed a couple cups of coffee before she could achieve anything close to a sparkle in hers.

"Hi, Al. I'm sorry to wake you. Are you okay?"

His expression said to her: *Think nothing of it, my dear. I was just getting up to start a busy day.*

Gina didn't see the notebook, or the pad of paper, either. She said a silent prayer. Funny how your future could ride on how fastidious a homeless man was. She drew in a breath.

"Al." She spoke gently. He looked at her with a quizzical, almost expectant look.

"Last night I may have left a notebook, maybe with the pad of paper you didn't want. Do you know where it is? Have you seen it?" Gina clung to the hope.

Al looked like he savored the moment. He smiled and burrowed back into his nest of blankets. Gina saw only Al's baggy pants-clad rump while he pawed under the blankets. Her heart pounded when he began to back out. Al sat up and thrust his arms forward with pride. The missing notebook was in his hands. For an instant, he looked just like that picture in her bedroom.

Gina's heart leapt and she leaned forward, kissed Al on his grimy cheek and gave him a big bear hug. Before she let go, Al whispered a single word. She thought it sounded like "Shaffer-hoont," but couldn't be sure.

"What was that, Al?" He sat with a beatific smile on his face. No answer.

"Stay right there, Al." Where was he going? "I'll be right back with breakfast. You're a lifesaver!"

Al looked like he was going to burst out laughing.

She hid the notebook in her big bag and hurried into the school building. The guards waved her through. Her shoulder muscles unbunched with relief.

The lab would be stocked with hot coffee and donuts. She even knew Al's favorites, with sprinkles and jelly filled.

Gina ducked into her office and tossed her notebook onto her desk where it flopped open. She turned to go back out the door and nearly ran over Dr. Choy.

"Careful, Gina!"

"Oh! Sorry Dr. Choy, I didn't see you. I was just going to share some of my breakfast with Al. Did you need to see me now?" She hoped he'd say no.

He smiled. "Later, yes? Go." Dr. Choy was an early riser, and when he was stumped tended to wander the halls and drop in on the staffers.

DR. CHOY leaned in the doorway to Gina's office and stared into space. He listened to the click of Gina's shoes. She carried a cardboard tray with goodies for the vagrant she had adopted. He looked down at the notebook that stood out among the otherwise orderly desk area. His eyes were drawn from the neat script he recognized as Gina's on one page, to text and symbols in multiple colors written in another hand. Curious, he stepped closer. The broken English he spoke and never bothered to correct belied a strong command of several languages, spoken and written. He stared in disbelief and turned pages at an increasing pace. He skimmed to the end and the realization hit him all at once. He ran out of the office and down the hall.

Dr. Choy pounded up the stairs and burst into the morning sun. He ran down the block and slowed only when he saw Gina standing, tray still in her hands, and a look of disbelief on her face.

"He's gone." She frowned. "I was just here, I don't understand."

They stood for a moment in silence then Dr. Choy nodded to himself. He took Gina by the arm and led her back to the lab.

GINA THOUGHT the weeks after the discovery of "The Shepherd" were positively dreamlike. She was still in shock that Al had literally vanished in the short time it took her to get him breakfast.

Al may have been gone, but he was far from forgotten. The day he left, Dr. Choy recognized an elaborate genetic design scrawled in Gina's notebook. When they returned to the lab, he and Gina read the section titled "Schaferhund" – the German word for shepherd.

The notebook contained complex genetic structures and detailed instructions on how to create and cultivate a designer virus. This one, which the scientists agreed to name *Shepherd*, served as a counter-measure to *the Wolf*. Like *the Wolf*, this virus was capable of disguising itself; in this case, it attacked *the Wolf* virus without triggering a response from it.

Shepherd also appeared effective in rooting out *the Wolf* in its earliest stages. It even served as a limited vaccine. For the first time in far too long, the teams combating the scourge of *the Wolf* allowed themselves to feel optimistic.

Gina never saw Al again. She would always remember him as Al, despite the carefully printed note at the end of the formula in her notebook. Dr. Choy translated it from German: *Gina, you were kinder to me than I deserved. Perhaps this will balance the scales a bit. - W.K.*

She didn't want to speak to the spate of government agencies eager to learn all about Al. She heard helicopters for days after the discovery. In the end, she was glad her responses disappointed the faceless agents, but she told the truth and the interrogations tapered off. She kept the memory of Al's expression the last time she saw him to herself. Wherever he was, she hoped he was at peace.

TRANSFUSIONS
JM
REINBOLD

It was 3 a.m. Will Diamond's daughter was dying and there was nothing he could do to save her. Not knowing what else to do, he had come to the hospital Chapel to pray. He was on his knees staring blindly at the carpet under the pews feeling confused and uncertain. There was no cross; in fact, there were no religious symbols at all. He asked a night duty nurse about it, and she told him it was because the Chapel was for patients and visitors of all faiths, not just Christians. Four walls of magnificent stained glass depicting children frolicking in gardens and wooded glades surrounded him. The pastoral scenes were meant to soothe and comfort, but Will, trying to find words to ask for a miracle from a God he hadn't acknowledged in years and wasn't even sure he believed in, barely noticed the vibrant colors. He made a few false starts before realizing he had no idea what to say. He thought for a few minutes, and then with sweaty palms pressed tightly together he tried again. "Please God, please save her. She needs a miracle. "

When he was done, it occurred to him that in his entire life he had done little or nothing for God, and so perhaps he had no right to expect God to do anything for him. "I'll go to church," he promised, "I'll go to church, and I'll take Susan and make sure she goes to Sunday school. And," he added with a sigh, "I'll read the Bible, too." Will groaned. What a pathetic prayer. He rested his forehead on his clenched hands. Tears leaked from the corners of his eyes. Finally, he gave in to desperation. "Listen," he said, half choking out the words. "Listen, I'll do anything. There must be something. Anything. Whatever you need; I'll do it. Please, please, just save my little girl."

WILL AWOKE with a jolt. He felt like he'd just been body slammed into the pew. His heart was racing and a bullet of panic was ricocheting around inside his head. For a few moments he had no idea where he was. He gripped the pew in front of him and tried to calm himself down. *Take it easy; just take it easy.* It was only a dream. Some dream; he couldn't remember when he'd been so scared. He sat up and rubbed the sleep out of his eyes. Scratching the stubble on his cheeks, he wondered how long he'd been asleep. The dream memories were beginning to slip away. The last thing he remembered was praying. And, he had a hazy recollection of talking to someone. He didn't have time to worry about it now. He checked his wristwatch. 8 a.m. He couldn't believe it. He'd been asleep for five hours. A blast of adrenalin roused him. He had to get back to Susan. What if she'd woken up and found him gone? What if she needed him? He pushed through the Chapel doors and ran through a maze of corridors to his daughter's room.

WILL LURCHED forward and nearly fell off his chair. He had dropped off again. The nightmare he'd had earlier was still churning around in his head. He remembered that the person he'd been talking to was a fierce looking old man with long, white hair and an equally long beard. But his appearance kept changing – first male, then female, young, old, middle-aged, and he kept changing race and ethnicity, too – never staying the same for more than a few seconds, and finally becoming nothing Will recognized as human, just colors, smells, sounds and shifting patterns of light. Sometimes it spoke, and sometimes he felt its thoughts in his head. Then he was standing on a stage, like he'd had to do at high school graduation. He wanted to run away, but above him a powerful light switched on leaving him exposed and vulnerable. Beyond the column of light he could see only shadows. Shadows that murmured and cried out as they pressed closer and closer. They were reaching for him, exuding a terrible longing that gripped him and drew him nearer and nearer the darkness. That's what had scared the bejesus out of him and woke him up. That and the blood. He remembered the blood and the awful, overwhelming anxiety flooding through him. He didn't want to think about blood. Blood had ruined his life. Blood was why his wife was dead and his daughter was dying, all because of a blood transfusion.

Will made a couple swipes through his sparse, sand colored hair. The chair he was sitting in was beyond uncomfortable. It was the kind of chair that if you fell asleep in it you'd wake up thinking you'd become a paraplegic. His butt and his right leg were numb, and the unpleasant deadening sensation had started to creep up the right side of his body. He pushed himself forward on the seat and stood up, gritting his teeth at the "pins and needles" as blood rushed back into his leg.

He looked down at Susan sleeping curled on her side. Careful not to wake her, Will smoothed her hair and fussed with the blanket. The pastel curtain divider was pushed back to the wall since, for the moment, Susan had no roommate. He was grateful for the cheerful colors and the cute animal wallpaper. There was a television, and some of Susan's drawings and the funny cards he'd brought her were pinned to a bulletin board across from her bed. The nurses had brought in a fold up cot for him to sleep on, but mostly he stayed in the chair beside her bed, because if Susan woke up Will wanted her to know right away that he was there.

Without insurance Will had no idea how he would pay for another hospital stay. It had taken him a while to realize there was no point in worrying. He didn't have a choice. He would just have to do what his friends and neighbors had been telling him to do and start a campaign or something to help with Susan's medical bills. Other people did it, so why not him? Right, Will thought, like he had any idea how to organize something like that. Katie could have done it. She was always raising money for some kind of cause. It was a shame that when she needed someone to champion her cause no one had come forward to help. Sighing, Will reached for a local newspaper lying on the rolling tray table at the foot of Susan's bed. He wondered where it came from. He guessed one of the night duty nurses must have forgotten it.

He leafed through the pages with little interest until an article near the back caught his eye: Local Evangelist Claims Faith-Healing Son Cured Man of AIDS. Will read the article in disbelief, punctuated with snorts of disgust. How could anyone be that sleazy? Making money from something as terrible as AIDS? It figured though, Will thought, if anyone would go that low it had to be those crack-pot fundies.

Will studied the photograph next to the article. The Rev. Everett J. Gamble and his son, Jimmy Gamble, stood in front of a tent that sported a gimmicky banner that read: Gamble on God – You Can't Lose! The evangelist and his son looked vaguely familiar, but Will couldn't imagine where he'd ever have seen them before. To Will the Rev. Gamble looked like the most dangerous species of used car salesman. The kind that had an obsessive and unshakable, if delusional, confidence in the junk he sold and the lies he told. Jimmy Gamble looked more like a rock star than Will's idea of a faith healer. Dark shoulder length hair spilled over his handsome face. His doe eyes were serious and a solemn contrast to his child-like smile. It was easier to imagine Jimmy Gamble clutching a microphone, supercharging the libidos of teenage girls, than ministering to the sick and crippled.

Will's skin prickled and a sudden dizziness made him sit up straight and grip the sides of the chair. It occurred to him that maybe this was God's way of helping Susan. "Jesus!" Will shuddered, and then quickly crossed himself. "Don't be an idiot." His recent tendency to talk to himself, and then answer himself disturbed him almost as much as the article about the evangelist and his son. Will had hardly slept since bringing Susan to the hospital. Maybe he was starting to lose it. He rammed the paper into the trash can, noticing at the same instant that Susan was awake, watching him.

"Good morning, sweetie." Will said, taking her hand in his.

"Hi, Daddy." Her voice was weak, but she was smiling again.

"Did I wake you up?"

Susan shook her head, no. "I was dreaming. The dream woke me up."

"I'm sorry you had a bad dream," Will said gently, "I had one, too."

Susan shook her head again. "It wasn't a bad dream, Daddy. I saw an angel. He kissed me and told me everything was going to be okay." Susan closed her eyes and smiled. "He had really pretty eyes."

Will's mind jumped at the idea. God sent angels, didn't He? "Did the angel say anything else?" Will asked.

Susan nodded. "He said I can go home now."

Will's heart sank. He should have known better. Susan had made up the angel. "Sweetie," Will said, "I know you don't like it here, but we're going to have to stay awhile." What did he expect? She was only eight and she wanted to go home.

A FEW hours later, Dr. Wilson, one of Susan's doctors, and the head of Pulmonology, told Will to take Susan home. At first Will was stunned, then outraged, but so bone tired he could barely muster the energy to protest.

"We've done all we can do, Mr. Diamond," Dr. Wilson said. "And, under the circumstances, given her condition when you brought her in, Susan has improved a great deal. I can't explain it. It's remarkable really. At any rate, she'll be better off at home. There's less chance of a secondary infection; she'll be in familiar surroundings, and being cared for at home is a lot less stressful for a child than a hospital stay." Dr. Wilson patted Will's shoulder. "We're always here if there's an emergency. I've already said goodbye to Susan. Call me if you need me, please." He walked away leaving Will feeling numb. Dr. Wilson was young and still earnest. Will knew that he cared, but what good was that to Susan. Her devoted young doctor couldn't cure her or even save her life.

Will's shoulder's sagged as he returned to his daughter's room feeling even more helpless than before. Susan was sleeping. He saw that the nurses had plaited her waist length blonde hair and tucked it inside her nightgown. Will's eyes stung at the sight of her bangs, uneven because she'd tried to trim them herself. The rise and fall of her chest was barely visible, and he leaned in close to make sure she was breathing.

He didn't want to disturb her; she needed her rest, as much of it as she could get. That was a sad situation for an eight-year-old. Will sighed as he bent over the narrow bed and kissed Susan's forehead, glad for the first time that her mother wasn't alive to see their daughter stricken with an incurable illness, and her husband barely able to cope. *Don't dwell on it. You're all Susan's got now.* The reality of it made him cringe. *And she's all you've got, so get yourself together, or you might as well not even be around.* But he couldn't help feeling that no matter what he did things just got worse instead of better. He'd always relied on Katie to know the right thing to do. "One thing at a time," Will said to himself. That's what Katie always told him. "Take a deep breath and just take one thing at a time."

After he'd thought about it for a while, Will decided Dr. Wilson was right. It would be a good thing to take Susan home from the hospital, away from the cute room that could never feel like home, the ever-present smell of disinfectant, and the constant monitoring of the nurses. Susan had improved a lot. Dr. Wilson had said so. So while Susan slept, he packed the nightgowns and sweaters he'd brought for her, trying to do it like her mother would have done it, everything folded properly and stacked correctly.

WILL HADN'T expected to bring Susan home so soon. There wasn't much food in the house and even though he didn't like leaving her alone, he'd settled her on the couch in front of the TV and run down the street to the Quickie Market to grab a few things for dinner. Guilt swept over him as he finished filling their dinner plates with Hamburger Hot Meals. There hadn't been much of a selection and he wasn't much of a cook. It was hard for Will to look at his daughter without getting choked up. She was small for her age and very thin. And if that wasn't bad enough, since they'd gotten home she hadn't been herself. But Will couldn't put his finger on what was different. Staring blankly through the kitchen window, it suddenly occurred to him that Susan knew she was going to die. The thought chilled him. She'd never mentioned it, never asked him anything. He wasn't even sure she knew what death was. It took Will the better part of thirty minutes before he felt able to face her. He reheated their plates in the microwave, then put on a pretend smile as he carried them into the living room.

He'd left Susan stretched out on the couch watching Ancient Mysteries. He was surprised by her choice of programs. Only a few days ago, before she'd gone to the hospital, she wanted to watch Scooby Doo and Nickelodeon, and she'd acted like an eight-year-old, laughing at Scooby's antics and calling Will every five minutes to come and see. But today she'd selected Secrets of the Dead and re-runs of Strange Luck and the X Files, shows she'd never had any interest in before. Will wondered if he should stop her from watching some of the stuff. But he didn't have the heart to object. It doesn't matter what she watches, Will thought, saddened by the realization, it doesn't matter at all. Still, it was strange, the sudden change in her choice of programs, as if in a just a day she had grown older and more mature than her eight years. Where was his Susan, his little girl? He could no longer find her in the ancient child that looked back at him, eyes dark and impenetrable with a wisdom he couldn't comprehend.

Will looked around their cramped living room. Ancient Mysteries was still on the television, but the couch was empty. Susan's pink comforter, embroidered with dancing ponies, was in a heap on the floor.

"Susan," Will called. "Where are you, honey? Dinner's ready." Will expected to hear Susan holler "Okay, Daddy!" from the other side of the bathroom door, but there was no answer.

"Susan?" Will called again, louder. Again there was no answer. Will set the plates on the glass-topped coffee table. "Susan! Susan!" he shouted, trying to suppress the panic creeping into his voice.

"Coming, Daddy," Susan answered.

Will felt light-headed and realized he'd been holding his breath. "Take it easy, guy," he said quietly. "Just settle down." He pulled in a few slow, deep breaths and followed Susan's voice down the hall and into her bedroom.

Like nearly everything of Susan's, her room was pink and decorated with glittery princesses, ponies and teddy bears. The window was open and the lace sheers were floating, lifted by a gentle, steady breeze. Susan was in her nightgown sitting on the edge of her bed. She stared intently at a newspaper, her eyebrows knotted in concentration.

"What are you doing, sweetie?" Will asked looking over her shoulder. Susan jumped and the paper dropped from her hands. Will came around the side of the bed and knelt to retrieve the paper. As he handed it back to her, he recognized the picture of Everett and Jimmy Gamble.

Startled, he asked, "Where did you get that?" It looked like the same paper he'd been reading at the hospital, but he was sure he'd thrown it out.

"It was in my suitcase," Susan replied without looking up.

Will sat down next to her. His skin prickled with goose bumps as he watched Susan tracing the outline of Jimmy Gamble's face.

He'd been so preoccupied with that stupid nightmare and with Dr. Wilson deciding to send Susan home, that maybe he just thought he threw the paper out. Will scratched his head. He could have set the paper down and piled Susan's clothes on top of it, then picked it up without realizing when he was packing her suitcase.

"Read this to me, Daddy." She held up the paper so he could see it and pointed to the article next to the picture of the Gambles. When he reached for the paper she wouldn't let him take it. Will thought she looked feverish. He pressed his hand against her forehead. She didn't feel hot.

"Susan, those are bad people."

She grabbed his arm. Her face was shiny with sweat. "Daddy, what does it say?"

Susan's agitation unsettled him. He was afraid he would upset her even more if he refused.

"'Local evangelist, the Rev. Everett J. Gamble, of the Church of Jesus Christ Sanguis Renascent, out of Blue Rock, MD,'" Will began, stumbling over the Latin words, "'has come under fire by local ministers and community health organizations because of his claims that his, eighteen-year-old son, alleged faith healer, E. J. "Jimmy" Gamble, Jr., cured a man of AIDS. Asked the identity of the man, Gamble refused to divulge his name insisting the man wished to remain anonymous and not have his 'miracle of blessedness' turned into a three ring circus by the media. Gamble's critics condemn his claims as self-serving, publicity seeking, and an attempt to financially exploit people desperate for any hope of a cure. Members of Gamble's church, however, were ready and willing to endorse his claims, but son, Jimmy, Jr., refused to comment.'"

WILL STOPPED reading at the end of the paragraph about the Gambles, although the article continued describing other self-proclaimed miracle workers and their outlandish claims. Susan pulled open the drawer of her bedside table, folded the paper and placed it inside.

"Susan, why do want to save that?" Will asked.

"We have to go there, Daddy," she said, closing the drawer firmly.

Will could have kicked himself for not noticing he'd put that paper in Susan's suitcase. "That's not a good idea ..." Will began, but stopped abruptly at his daughter's reaction. Susan's mouth turned down in distress. Her face was pale, her voice strained. She grabbed his arm again.

"We have to go, Daddy. I have to see Jimmy!" She was crying and shaking, her breathing ragged.

Will put his arms around her and hugged her, trying to comfort her.

"Okay," he said stroking her hair, "we'll go. We'll talk about it some more tomorrow, okay?"

Susan nodded. She struggled to take a deep breath and started to cough. Will rubbed her back hoping she would calm down and discovered her nightgown was damp. He got a fresh gown and helped her change. Then he propped her pillow against the headboard and helped her lean back.

"Did you forget about dinner?" Will asked, hoping he could change the subject. "I bet I have to heat it up again. Tell you what. I'll do that and then let's watch Baby Animals Just Want to Have Fun, okay? And guess what? I got Mr. Cookie Faces for dessert! How about that?"

"I'm not so hungry, Daddy. I want to go to sleep now, okay?"

"Don't you want any dinner at all?"

Susan shook her head no.

"Okay, I guess," Will said, not sure he should let her go to bed without eating something. He tucked the covers around her and gave her a kiss on the forehead. "I guess missing dinner just this once won't hurt," Will said, trying to keep the disappointment out of his voice.

He paused at the door before switching off the light. "Sleep tight. Don't let the bed bugs bite."

Susan giggled reassuring him that she was all right. He pulled the door shut behind him. "Holler if you need anything, okay?" he called through the crack.

Susan yawned. "Okay, Daddy, night-night."

Will walked back to the living room and clicked off the TV. He picked up Susan's comforter and tossed it on the couch, then gathered up their plates on his way to the kitchen. He covered Susan's plate with plastic wrap and put it in the 'fridge then sat down at the kitchen table and ate his dinner cold. Why had he told Susan he would take her to that faith healer? Katie always knew what to say to Susan. He was always making stupid mistakes. He hoped she would forget about it. Maybe if he slipped in during the night and took the paper away ... Will groaned. What if there was even the slightest chance? But that was crazy, wasn't it? As crazy as me praying for a miracle, he thought. He needed to talk to somebody, but who was there to talk to about something like that? Dr.

Wilson! He would call Dr. Wilson. He had helped Will before. That settled, Will decided to get a beer and sit out on the porch for a while and watch the world go by. With a much lighter heart, he went to the 'fridge to get his beer. Just as he was about to step out the kitchen door onto the porch, he thought he heard a noise. He shut the door and set his beer on the table. He'd better check on Susan. As he stepped from the dining room into the hall leading to the two bedrooms at the back of the house, Will was surprised to see bright light seeping out from around Susan's bedroom door. He hurried down the hall and tapped on the door.

"Susan? You okay?" She didn't answer. He opened the door a crack and peeked inside. He had expected the light to be on, but the room was dark, lit only by the pale glow of the night light. It took a few seconds for his eyes to adjust. Susan appeared to be sleeping peacefully, but he went in and looked just to be sure, and saw he'd forgotten to close the window. Katie would have kicked his butt for not taking care of it before he tucked Susan in. He shut the window and locked it. As he turned to leave, he glanced at the drawer of the nightstand. He could probably get it open, take the paper, and close the drawer again without waking Susan. And what if she did wake up? He didn't want her to have another meltdown like the one earlier. He decided not to risk it and left, shutting the door without a sound. On his way back to the kitchen, Will turned and looked at Susan's door. No sign of the light he'd seen just moments before. He turned off the overhead light in the dining room and looked again. Nothing. Was he seeing things now? He shook his head. Susan must have had her light on, and then turned it off right before he opened the door. Was she pretending to be asleep? Why would she do that? Maybe she'd been looking at that picture again and didn't want him to know. That must be what happened. He would talk to Dr. Wilson about it tomorrow; he'd know what to do. Back in the kitchen, Will picked up his beer and headed out to the porch.

SUSAN LAY quietly in the darkness, fingers clutching reflexively at her light blanket as she listened to her father's footsteps retreating down the hallway. When his footfalls were silenced by the dining room carpet, she let a few more minutes pass before she pushed herself up on one elbow and opened the drawer of the bedside table. Susan removed the folded newspaper and hugged it to her chest. She shut the drawer and rolled back into the softness of her bed.

On and off all day she'd had a funny feeling like someone was watching her. Sometimes she felt like someone was right next to her, close enough to touch. While her father was cooking dinner she'd been watching a television program where a boy was calling for his sister. She heard him say, "Susan, Susan!" But his sister's name wasn't Susan. Then she'd heard it again and thought it must be her father calling her. She went to the kitchen, but he was busy at the stove, and when she heard the voice again it was coming from the back of the house. Following the voice to her room, she had the feeling again of someone close by. The room was too warm and she'd opened the window. Someone was standing by the broken lamppost across the street on the path that cut through the hedge, at least she thought so. But when she looked again no one was there, only the long, untrimmed branches swaying in the breeze.

Lying in bed, she felt the closeness again like a pressure in the air around her. Now it felt familiar, something she recognized. "Are you here?" she whispered to the darkness.

It didn't happen right away, first there was the light. The bright golden light; so bright she had to cover her eyes. The light was seeping into her like drops of sweat squeezing through her pores, only from the outside in. She opened her eyes just enough to peek through her fingers. It was him! The angel she'd seen in her dream at the hospital; the angel that brought the light. At least she thought he was an angel, but she wasn't sure because he didn't have wings. Smiling, Susan closed her eyes. She felt like she was floating, like milkweed floss riding on a breeze. The golden light filled her from head to toe, and nothing anywhere in her whole entire being hurt. She felt her heart pulsing and at its center a warm swirl of something that sounded like voices and felt like music, something that became a tiny, bright kernel of secret knowledge that made her gasp.

She sensed the light outside her fading, but not inside. Inside she felt like a blazing star or a newborn sun, and she knew what she had to do. She slid the page of newspaper under her pillow. Snuggling deep into her blanket she whispered a prayer. "Now I lay me down to sleep. I pray the Lord my soul to keep. If I die before I wake, I pray the Lord my soul to take." After a slight pause she added, "I'll be there soon, and I'm not afraid."

WILL WALKED around their '77 Plymouth Fury. The car had sat idle in a garage for years before Will bought it from a neighbor clearing out after his father died. Once a dark metallic green, the years had faded the paint to a nondescript shade of lime. The car was fine for going to the grocery store, or back and forth to the doctor, but it wasn't the kind of vehicle he wanted to take on a road trip. Sure, he'd put new tires on it after that near miss they'd had last winter, but the wheels were out of alignment, and the thing vibrated like an overloaded washing machine if he went over 30 mph. There was no spare tire and the speedometer hadn't worked in six months. And if that wasn't enough, the car was covered with dents and dings. Out on the Interstate they'd be a cop magnet for sure. Will rubbed the back of his neck. The Fury looked like he felt; it had seen better days. No way, Will thought, no way am I driving this car out of state. Damn it, he'd just have to put his foot down.

The back door opened with a shrill squeak and then banged shut.

"Daddy," Susan called. She was coming across the yard struggling into the straps of her teddy bear backpack. "Are you ready to go?" She was dressed in her best embroidered jeans and the pink t-shirt and jacket set with the sparkly buttons she'd gotten for her birthday. A frilly pink scrunchy held her ponytail in place. She had on her new sneakers, too; the one's with the red lights in the heels that blinked when she walked. Will was startled to see that she was wearing pink lip-gloss, until he remembered that their neighbor, Mrs. Cebenka, had given Susan some of her Avon samples to play with. Will hesitated for a moment, looked at the car, then back at Susan.

"Ready!" he called, trying to sound cheerful. He opened the door for her, helped her climb into the low seat then fastened her seat belt. He went around to the driver's side, got in, and belted up. They pulled out of the yard and drove the few miles to the Interstate entrance ramp with the exhaust manifold thwacking like a boat propeller every time Will accelerated.

HEADING SOUTH on 1-95 Will relaxed a little. Moving along at a steady 55 mph the Fury sounded pretty good. Well, it sounded better anyway. Susan had dozed off within minutes of getting on the Interstate, succumbing to the smooth, uninterrupted movement of the car, leaving Will to his own thoughts. He had called Dr. Wilson and asked him to talk to Susan and tell her that going to a faith healer was a bad idea. But Dr. Wilson let him down. "Susan's eight years old," he'd told Will, "if she wants to do something you don't think is safe, then it's up to you to tell her no." Before Will had a chance to reply, Dr. Wilson proceeded to tell him that he'd heard of people being cured of rheumatoid arthritis, paralysis, and even cancer by faith healers.

"You can't be serious!" Will said.

"I'm not saying the faith healers have anything to do with it," Dr. Wilson said. "I don't claim to be able to explain the phenomena. The human mind is an incredible thing; it's entirely possible that these folks heal themselves; I just don't know. But at this point it can't hurt to give it a try."

Will still couldn't believe he'd agreed to take Susan to a faith healer or how insistently she had pestered him to take her. He talked to her about it again, explaining why it was a bad idea, doing his best to make her understand that what faith healers did wasn't real. But Susan had begged and pleaded, then burst into tears. And Will, unable to bear seeing her so distraught, had caved in a second time and promised to take her to Jimmy Gamble. In the end, it had just seemed easiest to let her find out for herself, and hope that the experience wouldn't be too traumatic. On the other hand, as much as he hated to admit it, maybe Dr. Wilson had a point. Maybe Susan would be one of those people who healed herself. But she was just a kid. How did a thing like that happen anyway? Will didn't believe it could happen. So what had he expected when he prayed for a miracle? Something quiet, Will thought. Susan wakes up one morning and she's well. The disease is gone, no fanfare, no faith healers, no one can explain it. It's a miracle and that's that. Everybody's life goes back to normal.

THEY HAD been on the road four and a half hours. Will had no idea where they were, except that they were somewhere in the bowels of Maryland. He'd given himself an extra half hour in case they got lost, and now that was gone. Will grimaced. The gas was going to cost him a fortune, and worse, he was afraid the trip would exhaust Susan. They had been up and down this section County Road 85 at least six times. There was no other turn except a dirt road with a hand painted sign that dog-legged off of it. Every time they passed that road Susan grabbed at Will's shirt and pointed at the sign.

"Daddy! Daddy!" she shouted. "That's the road. That's the road!"

Out of patience, Will hollered, "Susan! That road isn't even on the map."

She was driving Will crazy. He couldn't figure out how she'd gotten it in her head that a road that looked like a dirt bike trail was the road they were looking for. Ever since Susan had woken up she'd been agitated and acting peculiar. Will couldn't understand it, and he was getting increasingly anxious worrying that this sudden burst of energy was some strange precursor to another decline in her health.

Susan grabbed the steering wheel and jerked it toward her side of the car. The Fury veered sharply to the right almost running into a ditch. Will hit the brakes and pulled back on the wheel just as the front passenger side tire left the pavement. Heart pounding like a jackhammer, Will stared at his daughter in disbelief. But Susan wasn't looking at him. Her eyes were fixed on the dirt road. The feverish look from the day before had returned, and the knuckles of her hands, still clutching the steering wheel, were chalk white.

Will wanted nothing more than to go home, but was afraid of how Susan would react. Not knowing what else to do, he said, "Okay, okay, we'll try the dirt road." Susan settled back in her seat. Will put the car into reverse and checked the rearview and sides mirrors before backing up. He hesitated a moment and looked at Susan before shifting into Drive.

"Hurry, Daddy," she said, "or we'll miss the service." Her voice sounded calmer now and Will hoped there'd be no more surprises.

He gave the car some gas and turned onto the dirt road. It was starting to get dark, and he had to squint to see the hand painted sign: Purgatory Swamp Road. It had to be a joke! Still, he didn't like the sound of it, or the look of it. And he certainly didn't like the idea of driving it in the dark.

"Jesus!" Will said out loud. He looked over at Susan. She had unhooked her seat belt and pulled herself up to the dashboard.

"Susan," Will said, "put your seatbelt back on, right now."

She turned to look at Will. "This is the way, Daddy," Susan cried, pointing down the darkening road. In the dim light her pale blue eyes looked silver.

Will wanted to stop and get Susan back into her seat belt, but there was no shoulder and he had to keep a tight grip on the steering wheel to keep control of the Fury as it rocked and thudded its way over the deeply rutted road. Over-hanging tree branches prevented most of the moon's light from illuminating the surrounding area, and Will hoped they didn't have much further to go before connecting with a real road. They were just crawling along. Were the headlights getting dimmer? He could hardly see a thing.

"Whoa!" Will shouted. For a moment his stomach felt like it was hanging in mid-air. He'd felt the absence of road just before the left front wheel crashed down into a pot hole.

He turned to Susan, "You okay, honey?"

Susan nodded, "I'm okay, Daddy. Is the car okay?"

Will pressed the gas pedal. The engine revved, but the Fury didn't budge. He pressed harder with same result.

"Oh no," Will whispered.

He heard the passenger side door handle clunk. Startled, he turned to see Susan clambering out of the car.

"Susan!" Will shouted. "Susan, wait!"

Frantically pumping his door handle, he discovered that the door was jammed shut. Will scrambled over the seats and out onto the road. He caught a glimpse of Susan's blond hair in the headlights. She had started walking. He could see the red lights in her sneakers flashing.

"Susan!" Will shouted. "Susan!" His voice sounded shrill and hysterical. If she went much further she'd be out of sight. With panic mounting, he started after her and almost immediately stumbled into a rut and twisted an ankle. He winced at the pain ricocheting around his foot. Hauling himself up, he gritted his teeth and limped along as quickly as he could, his ankle straining against the extra weight he'd piled on. How could Susan move so quickly without falling? Why didn't she wait for him? Then he heard her voice just up ahead.

"Come one, Daddy! Come on. We have to hurry or we won't get there in time!"

Relieved, Will realized Susan had turned around. That's why he couldn't see the red lights in her shoes.

"Susan!" Will shouted. "I'm coming, honey. Just stay where you are."

Further along the road he heard a roaring noise. He couldn't be sure, but he thought the sound was ahead of him. It swelled up then dropped away. When the wind was at his back, he couldn't hear it at all, but then, when the wind shifted, the sound swelled up again louder than before. An odd wailing sound that reminded Will of a shrieking train whistle stopped him in his tracks. "What in the world is that?" he wondered out loud as he slapped at the mosquitoes whining around his head.

STANDING ON the steps of his touring bus, the Rev. Everett Gamble admired the rosy glow of sunset reflected on the white canvas of his new revival tent. Even with the stage, runway and audio equipment set up it could still hold two hundred people. It had taken ten or twelve men from his congregation most of the morning to erect it in the field out back of the Hunter's Lodge motel.

Stuart and Gladys Arniss, the motel's owners, were members of Everett's church. A few years back they had come up to Blue Rock and Jimmy had healed Gladys of rheumatoid arthritis. Needless to say, when Everett took the ministry on the road, the Arniss's were more than willing to let Everett hold revival meetings at their place outside of Rock Hall, and they didn't charge him a dime. Hell, having meetings here was the best thing ever came their way. They cleaned up renting rooms to folks who came from a distance to see Jimmy, and they had a restaurant and a Bible shop out on the highway to boot.

When Everett first brought the meetings to Hunter's Lodge the motel looked rundown and weedy. Its clientele consisted of hunters in the fall and winter, fisherman in the spring and summer, and couples year round who were looking for an out of the way place they could rent for an hour or two. Nowadays, Hunter's Lodge was looking clean and respectable. 'Welcome, friend' was painted on the glass in the office door, and on the highway side a neon cross glowed comfortingly alongside the 'Vacancy' sign, informing motorists they were approaching an oasis for the Christian traveler.

Times were looking up for the ministry, too. Everett had a permanent building in Blue Rock where he held two services every Saturday and Sunday. But he couldn't get the road out of his blood, and his traveling ministry had expanded his congregation and his reputation. Why only a month ago he'd traded up to this new two-hundred person tent and, with eyes always on the future, he had just this morning set his sights on a massive thousand-person cathedral tent. He gazed out at the field, his imagination overlaying the scene with the new pavilion, shining white and many-peaked, rising out of the grass like a vision of the New Jerusalem. Just the thought of it took his breath away.

He could hear cars pulling into the parking lot in a steady stream. Shaking off his daydream, he looked down the hill at the dark tangle of trees and swamp below and shivered. The tree frogs and crickets had begun their night-long chirping. In the far woods owls were hooting. He looked up when the sodium lights in the parking lot came on around him. Bats were swooping and diving, hunting the insects that swarmed in the orange-yellow halos surrounding the lamps. He breathed in deeply and took a last look at the distant fields beyond the tent. Above the unmown grass fireflies winked on and off like stars fallen down from the heavens. He checked his watch. 7:55 p.m. He'd better get a move on.

AT THE back of the stage, Everett scanned the crowd through a gap in the curtains. He reckoned that members of his church counted for at least half the congregation on any given night. The rest, the afflicted, were coming in on crutches, in wheel chairs and supported on the arms of friends and relatives. They had heard about Jimmy and come, some from hundreds of miles away, to be healed. Everett was uneasy, but he put it down to nerves. The same nerves he had every night until he stepped on the stage and grabbed his microphone. Then he pulled out his linen handkerchief and let the Spirit do the rest.

It was early. The crowd was fresh. It was the time Everett savored most, when he could bring all the power and passion of his faith to bear on them and whip them into a vigor that commanded God's attention. A few stragglers were still coming in, milling around, looking for chairs, but most were in their seats looking expectantly at the stage. It was time to get the show on the road. Everett swept the curtain aside. The choir, used to his explosive entrances, burst into song. He walked across the stage and grabbed the microphone from its stand. As he strode down the runway, people were already getting to their feet. Everett pulled his white linen handkerchief from his sleeve, a signal to the choir to conclude the hymn on the current verse. After greeting the congregation, he raised both arms and shouted, "Praise God! Praise God! Praise God Almighty! You are my witnesses, sisters and brothers! The Spirit of God will enter into us here tonight!" Hands shot into the air. Voices shouted, "Yes, Lord. Please, Lord."

That was Everett's cue. He filled up on air and let loose. "We live in dangerous times brothers and sisters. Dangerous times. We know them to be the end times. And we know the signs. We know that it's now or never to get right with God. Every day we are tempted. Every day it is harder to see evil for what it is. Every day our lives, our eternal souls are in deadly peril. We no longer fear only the transgressions of men, but the final onslaught of the legions of Hell. That onslaught has one single, unrelenting purpose. And that purpose is to drag down and destroy those whose faces are turned toward heaven in rapture!"

After exhorting the congregation for another hour, Everett had perspired through his suit and needed a change of clothes. He could hear the big air handlers running, but the place still stank of sweat and disease.

Everett signaled the choir, already champing at the bit, to lay into a hymn that would rock the place off its pegs. The words flashed across screens above him, but most knew the hymns by heart. In the congregation, a woman, her thin flower print dress damp and clinging to her body, stomped and clapped, wailing her lungs raw on sweet Jesus.

The unease Everett had felt earlier plagued him through the whole service. It was not the familiar anxiety that caused him to pace incessantly like a caged animal, but an odd sense of portentousness. He might even call it foreboding. Everett had not experienced anything like it since the day Jimmy was born. But nothing unusual had happened. He looked over his shoulder. And there, at the far right of the stage, out of sight of the congregation, stood Jimmy looking straight at him.

Everett rubbed his chin. Just this morning he'd nicked himself a good one while shaving. The cut was deep, and even with a tab of tissue stuck on the wound, he was still oozing blood when he'd gone into the buses' dining area to have breakfast with Jimmy. The boy had noticed the cut right away, touching Everett's chin so lightly he'd hardly felt it. Then, before Everett had a chance to pick up his fork, Jimmy had commenced to worry him with a whole litany of concerns about the ministry. This had been going on for a few months, ever since Jimmy turned eighteen, and Everett was heartily tired of it. He'd gotten up without touching his food and walked out.

In the preceding seventeen years of his life Jimmy had done exactly what Everett told him to do. He had never had one minute of trouble from the boy, not one. And now it wasn't even cars or women or what have you. Jimmy had challenged Everett's ministry. He was haranguing him about healing souls. Pestering him about something he called the Ascension. Said he didn't want to keep healing people's bodies if he couldn't mend their souls. "You start doing that," Everett told him, "and you'll put every preacher in the country out of business." Hells bells, God in heaven, Everett thought, no telling what kind of trouble that could start. He had always assumed it was evil that would bring about the end of the world, but, now he thought about it, he reckoned an over abundance of goodness might lead to the same result. Everett screwed up his face like something foul had just been placed under his nose. God had given Jimmy the gift of healing, Everett didn't dispute it for a minute, but the boy was no prophet. No sir. That was Everett's territory, and he'd be damned if he was going to let Jimmy step all over him.

Later, when he'd looked in the bathroom mirror there was no sign of the cut. His chin was as clear and unmarked as before he'd shaved.

The boy was good to him that was sure enough. Since he and Jimmy had been together Everett had not experienced a day of illness, not even a head cold. He'd gotten used to never feeling an ache or a pain, never having a toothache or even a cavity. Everett sighed. Truth be told, he needed Jimmy to draw the crowds. The boy was a miracle man and knew it.

As the thunder of heavenly voices surged up around him, Everett nodded to Jimmy. Turning back to the congregation his amplified voice swelled above the crowd.

"You need to be strong. You need the healing power of God Almighty to bind together the infirmities of your body and knit your flesh into armor invincible against Satan. I know who you need. I know who you came to see."

Jimmy Gamble walked onto the stage. The crowd roared. He paused as hands began to reach out, timidly at first, then with increasing boldness. Then he smiled and stepped off the stage and went out among the people.

"Can you feel the power of God that fills him?" Everett's voice rose above the tumult. "Look at him!" Everett shouted. "Look at that face. The Holy Spirit has made him as beautiful to look upon as any angel! Draw your measure of God's healing Spirit! The true elixir of Life! Drink from the Lord's own fountain! Drink his pure, holy essence and live your lives abundant and whole!"

Everett watched as the crowd pressed forward. How did the boy know which ones to take hold of? But he did sure enough. He held their faces in his hands, shut his eyes and prayed over them. Everett could see his lips moving, but it was impossible hear with all the crying and moaning. After Jimmy healed them some fell to their knees and prayed. Others thrashed and writhed as if they were trying to expel demons. There seemed to be no end to them. Everett watched as they rose up around Jimmy like a human pyre aflame with the Holy Spirit.

WILL AND Susan emerged from under the canopy of trees into the moonlight to find Purgatory Swamp Road dead-ended in a pile of weed-choked debris. It looked as if someone had taken a bulldozer and scraped the rest of the road into a heap. Surrounded by wild grapevine, honeysuckle and sticker bushes, there was no getting past the obstruction except to climb over it. Frantic to get to the service, Susan was undeterred. Without a thought of what she might be getting into, she scrambled up the side of the pile. Before she disappeared over the top, Susan reached for Will, urging him on. With his mind conjuring images of broken glass, jagged metal and poisonous snakes he'd gotten down on his hands and knees in a hurry and crawled over the rubble.

Despite scraped knees and bruised elbows they made it over the pile and discovered a rough-cut field on the other side. In the near distance, Will saw lights and the dark shapes of buildings. Behind the buildings, across from what Will now realized must be a parking lot, a large pavilion spilled golden light. With its double-peaked top, it reminded him of a circus tent. They could hear music and singing, people shouting. Hot, dirty, and covered in sweat, Will brushed dirt and dried grass out of Susan's hair. Her ponytail was snarled with a clump of stickers he'd have to cut out later. He was exhausted, but Susan seemed far from tired. At first he'd been angry when she ran ahead. Now he was just confused. It didn't make sense. Sure Dr. Wilson said Susan was doing better, better than anyone could have predicted. He even admitted he couldn't explain it. But this? She was pulling on his arm now, tugging him into the field, toward the lights. He held her hand tightly as they set out across the field.

Anything was better than Purgatory Swamp and its legions of ravenous mosquitoes.

ON THE other side of the parking lot Will saw the road he'd spent all evening searching for. How could he have missed it? Just as visible was the sign for the Hunter's Lodge Motel, and next to it a flashing 'Vacancy' sign and tall neon cross. There was even a banner stretched above the entrance announcing the Gamble's Healing Ministry. When they reached the tent a mass of people were streaming out heading for their cars. Without realizing it Will relaxed his hold on Susan. Her fingers slipped from his hand and before he realized what was happening she ran into the midst of the crowd.

My God! She'll be trampled to death, Will thought, as he frantically limped after her. The faces of the people he bumped into, that pushed and jostled him as he tried to catch up to Susan, were all a blur. He couldn't get over how determined she was, pushing and shoving her way through the crowd. The noise was deafening, but the heat and smell were worse. Just when he thought he couldn't endure it another minute, Will stumbled through the last of the departing faithful. The service was over. Jimmy Gamble was gone. Susan was staring at the stage, tears streaming down her face. Will stood there gasping. He wanted to bawl her out. Sick or not she needed a spanking. But by the time he'd caught his breath, the flare of anger had passed He knelt clumsily and hugged her.

"I'm sorry we missed him, sweetie." Will stammered. "There'll be another time ..."

Before he could finish, Susan bolted out of his arms and ran back to the entrance. She was outside before Will could get up. He struggled to his feet and staggered after her. When he caught sight of her again, she was dodging between moving cars.

"Susan!" he screamed, charging after her despite the pain in his ankle. The side of a big Cadillac grazed Will's left hip and spun him around. The driver blared the horn as the car swept past. Lame on both sides now, Will was afraid his legs would give out. He jumped when Susan grabbed his hand.

"Come on, Daddy!" She hung on Will's arm pulling him along a line of cars parked in front of the guest rooms at the back of Hunter's Lodge.

Halfway down the line of cars, Will looked back over his shoulder and saw two touring buses, motors running, parked by the tent. The Church of Jesus Christ Sanguis Renascent was painted in a red italic script on their sides. As Will watched one of the buses pulled away, lumbering through the parking lot and out onto highway. Susan was still pulling him along and when she turned into an empty parking space between two new looking Cadillacs, Will tripped over a cement parking barrier. He kept his footing as he stumbled forward, preventing himself from running into an ice machine, but he couldn't help colliding with the wall between two guest rooms.

"Are you okay, Daddy?" Susan asked as she stepped onto the sidewalk in front of the numbered red doors

"No harm done I guess," Will said, rubbing his shoulder.

With only the slightest hesitation Susan turned right. Will followed her as she retraced their steps back two doors and stopped in front of room number 11.

"Here!" Susan said. She was flushed again and her breathing sounded ragged. Will was sure she was close to collapsing. Whatever was causing this manic energy was keeping her going, but it couldn't last. Her body would give out and then what? He had to get himself together. His brain was on overload; he couldn't think straight. Every time he'd tried to stop and gather his thoughts, the next thing he knew he was rushing headlong out of control again, like a movie stuck on fast-forward.

Will looked around. "What's here?"

"Jimmy's here!" Susan said pointing at the door. She was hopping from one foot to the other, doing an excited little dance. "Knock on the door, Daddy! Knock on the door!"

"No, Susan," Will said. "We're leaving. Right now." Her small fist shot past him and pounded on the door. A few seconds later the lock turned, the door swung open and a wave of cool, refreshing air rolled over them. Will was stunned by the size of the man looking down at him. He was huge, bigger than a pro-football player or professional wrestler. His dark hair, full beard and mustache were neatly trimmed. The perfectly tailored suit couldn't hide the fact that his body was dense with muscle.

"Sorry to bother you," Will said, "I don't know if you can help ..."
The giant cut him off. "What do you want?"

"We got lost and missed the healing service..." Will began, but was cut off again.

"We'll be here again Wednesday night, or you can come up to Blue Rock tomorrow or Sunday." He stepped back inside and started to shut the door.

Will grabbed the handle. "Wait!" he cried, desperation making his voice shrill. "You don't understand!"

The knob jerked out of Will's hand. The door flew open and smacked the wall with a sharp crack. Will lurched forward and was immediately shoved backward. His arm felt like a rubber band about to snap.

"I'll tell you what I understand," the man growled, his face darkening. "I understand I have to half carry him back here every night after you people get done with him. He's so tired he can't hardly walk!"

"I understand you can't accept his blessing without trying to suck him dry. You pollute the river of your own faith and then you come here and want Jimmy to fix you up. He heals you from his pure, sweet spirit. And what do you give him in return?" The man's bright hazel eyes bored through Will. He slammed his hand against the doorjamb.

"You give him all the filth from your miserable lives, 'til he's sick as a dog from all your damn poison."

He thrust himself through the doorway. "Get the hell out of here."

Will staggered backwards into one of the poles that supported the canopy above the walkway. As the man leaned to the side, reaching for the door handle Will saw someone come into the room behind him.

"Who is it, Earl Dean?"

"Nobody," Earl Dean said over his shoulder as he backed through the doorway. "Don't concern yourself."

"Jimmy!"

Both Will and Earl Dean were startled by Susan's voice. She ran from behind Will, darted past Earl Dean, making a beeline for the sinewy, barefooted young man behind him.

Perplexed, Jimmy Gamble looked intently at Susan. She gazed up at him, eyes wide and adoring. Within seconds his confusion resolved into a knowing smile. "So that's what happened to you," he murmured. He dropped down on one knee and extended his hand. "Welcome home, little sister." Ignoring his proffered hand, Susan wrapped her arms around his neck and hugged him.

"Susan!" Will gasped. He started through the door. Earl Dean turned, blocking his way.

"Stay back from him!"

"It's all right, Earl Dean," Jimmy said, "let him come in."

Earl Dean looked unconvinced, but moved aside. Will crossed the room in two steps, took Susan by the hand and pulled her away from Jimmy Gamble. Earl Dean shut the door then sat on the couch where he could keep an eye on Will.

Will wasn't sure what he thought a faith healer should look like, but it wasn't Jimmy Gamble. Jimmy was lean and muscular, his dark, unruly hair held back with a bandana. His black jeans bunched up around his ankles. 'Believe' was scrawled across the front of his t-shirt. He had silver crosses in both ears. For God's sake, Will thought, his nose is pierced. He could see a ruby, like a drop of blood, glinting on the side of the boy's nose.

Will had had enough. He was bone tired and he hurt all over. The healing ministry, Earl Dean, and Jimmy Gamble all gave him the creeps. "Come on," Will said, herding Susan toward the door. "We're leaving."

"No, Daddy," Susan said. Her brow furrowed as she dug her heels in and tried to pull away.

"He's the angel I saw in the hospital. He made the golden light."

"What?" Will said, hardly able to believe what he'd just heard. Susan was looking at him as if he should know what she was talking about.

"How can you say that? You're being silly."

Susan's face crumpled and she started to cry. Will hadn't meant to sound harsh, and he reminded himself of why he agreed to bring Susan here in the first place.

"Look," Will said to Jimmy, "My name is Will Diamond and this is Susan. Not that it matters to any of you, but my daughter is dying and…" He choked up. He had never said 'my daughter is dying' out loud, to anyone. He'd never said it in front of Susan. In an instant Will's anger drained away.

"We heard you cured a man of AIDS, but …"

"But you didn't believe it."

Will hesitated. "No, I didn't" he said, "I don't."

The couch creaked. Earl Dean stood up. He walked over to Will. "I'm that man," he said, "and I've got the paperwork to prove it."

Will's brain was reeling. "If that's true," he said to Jimmy, "then cure my daughter. Please, that's all I want. I want my little girl to live."

"Mr. Diamond," Jimmy said, "Susan was healed the night you prayed in the hospital."

Will looked helplessly at Susan. "What? Why didn't you tell me?" Even as he asked the question, he realized how ridiculous it was. She didn't know what he'd done. Then it hit him.

"How'd you know about …?"

"She did tell you," Jimmy interrupted. "You didn't believe her and worse, you made her not believe."

Susan looked reproachfully at her father. "He came back, Daddy. The light was in my room." She turned to Jimmy. "But you're not really an angel. You're …" she struggled to find the words.

Jimmy smiled and stroked her hair. "Close enough," he said. Susan's look of puzzlement vanished. Her expression became tranquil. She looked completely at peace.

"What? Wait, you were in my house …?" Will felt like his brain was about to explode. He turned to Susan. "If you knew, why did you still want to come here?"

"Because, Daddy," Susan said, "Jimmy needs our help."

"Our help?" Will stared at Jimmy, his eyes narrowing with suspicion.

"If you knew I was all better, you wouldn't have come." Susan looked at Will fiercely. "You would have broken your promise."

"What?" Will said, "I didn't …"

"Yes, you did, Daddy, I heard you. You said you'd do anything if God cured me."

"Mr. Diamond," Jimmy said, "that man whose blood made your daughter sick was no ordinary man. He had wise blood. He could read people's souls. He felt their pain. He saw where they were broken. And if he'd listened to his blood, he could have helped them. But he got scared.

He couldn't bear what he knew. He discovered that using drugs silenced his blood. After that, when he looked at people or touched them he didn't feel anything. He didn't know anything. He was empty. Not long after, he got sick with AIDS. He didn't try to save himself and eventually he died. But his blood passed on to Susan."

"Wise blood," Will said, "what the hell are you talking about? Wait a minute. You know what? I don't even want to know."

Jimmy looked at Will forcing him to hold his gaze. "What do think the chances are of that happening, Mr. Diamond? One in a million? Two million? Maybe three? A man decides to give blood. Why? He doesn't know. And when does he decide to do it? At a time he doesn't and can't know about. That tiny little window of time when the infection he had couldn't be detected."

"It was a mistake," Will said woodenly, "someone made a mistake. That blood should have been thrown out."

"It would have been a tragedy if that blood had been destroyed," Jimmy said. "Wise blood gives the soul voice in the body. The person with wise blood can see far beyond himself. That person can know the unknowable. As it happens, that man was supposed to come here. He was the one I was waiting on. No mistake," he looked at Susan and smiled, "same blood, different body."

"You're crazy," Will said. He jerked open the door, picked Susan up and carried her out to the parking lot. Jimmy and Earl Dean followed them outside. It was only when Will saw the rows of cars tucked into their slots for the night and the distant white moon hanging high above them, that he realized they couldn't go anywhere. Their car was in a ditch in the middle of nowhere. They were stranded. This a motel, Will thought, relieved. We can stay here tonight. He would find the office, get a room and call a tow truck in the morning.

Susan was squirming in his arms. Keeping an eye on the two men, Will let her down, but kept a hold of her as they started toward the highway and the front of the motel. Gravel crunched and headlights flared as a car turned into the lane and came toward them. As the car got closer, Will was sure it was the Cadillac that had sideswiped him earlier. As he stepped out its way, he tried to get a look at the driver, but the dark glass revealed only his own reflected image. The car crept past him and turned into an empty parking spot. The door opened and Will recognized Everett Gamble as he got out and took in the scene.

"What's going on here?" Everett asked Jimmy.

"Tonight is the beginning of my ministry."

"You saying you're fixing to go out on your own?" Everett appeared unconcerned but his forehead glistened with sweat. "I say you can't. I say you stay right here with me."

"I'm eighteen," Jimmy said. "I'm legal; it's the law."

Everett screwed up his face and gave Jimmy a fierce look. "What about the law of obeying your father?"

Jimmy stuck out his chin and gave Everett look for look. "I am obeying my father."

"Something's gone to your head, son."

"We're going to give people something they can believe in," Jimmy said. "We're going to give them the greatest show on earth."

"How you figure to do that?" Everett asked.

"With magic."

Everett's eyes bulged in their sockets. "What the hell are you talking about? Have you lost your mind?"

"What does an illusionist do?" Jimmy asked them. He looked around from one to another. When no one replied, he shrugged and continued. "An illusionist creates illusions. He tells people right up front, 'I create illusions. I play with reality. I am going to fool you into believing that what I do is real.' People hear this, they know this, but they don't want to believe it. They want to believe what the illusionist is doing is real. They want to be amazed. They want to be awed. If they think he is fooling them they get angry. If they find out he is fooling them they get even angrier. But he's already told them from the beginning that he has set out to fool them. It doesn't matter. They want to believe."

"Illusions?" Everett said, leaning back against the side of the Cadillac, an amused smiled tweaking the corners of his mouth. "What kind of illusions?"

Earl Dean had gone back into the room and come out again with a pair of shoes and socks that he handed to Jimmy. Jimmy thanked him and sat down on the parking barrier. He pulled on the socks, nudged his feet into the black sneakers, laced them and stood up.

"Levitating in the air, walking on water, passing through a locked door." Jimmy's smile was wide, his eyes sparkled; he was almost laughing. "Maybe even raise the dead," he said with a sly wink at Will.

Everett was shaking his head furiously. "Now, just hold on ..." he started, but Jimmy cut his protest short.

"Right out in the street," Jimmy said, "right out in the middle of everybody." He lifted his arms over his head and did a quick turn on the toes of his sneakers, letting his arms drift gracefully down to his sides, palms facing out and to the front. He regarded each of them individually for a few seconds. He seemed calm, almost indifferent to their stunned expressions. He closed his eyes and let his head fall slowly forward. Arms hanging limp at his sides, he stood in that position without moving for a few minutes. Will started to back away, but Susan was like an anchor on his arm. She was staring intently at Jimmy and refused to budge. Will swung his free arm around Susan's waist and scooped her up. He didn't care if he had to walk back to Delaware. They were getting out now.

"No, Daddy!" Susan shouted, wriggling fiercely in his arms.

Susan's protest roused Everett. He shifted himself off the car, chuckled, and took a couple steps toward Jimmy. Both men stopped dead in their tracks as Jimmy's feet lifted off the ground. A whoosh of air escaped from Everett's lungs as if he'd been punched in the stomach. Susan dropped from Will's arms, unnoticed, and ran to Earl Dean. Will stood, his mouth hanging open, unable to utter a single word as he watched Jimmy Gamble rise in the air above the parking area, higher then the motel roof top, higher than the poles of the sodium lights. Jimmy's eyes were still closed, but he had lifted his head and tilted his face upward. He held his arms away from his body, palms facing up. His legs were crossed at the ankles, toes pointing down. A radiant golden light shimmered around his body. He hung there briefly, then slowly descended. As his feet touched the ground he opened his eyes. He stood there watching them, an amused smile on his face.

"Check for wires if you want," he said.

Will didn't move. But Everett rushed forward and ran his hands all over Jimmy's clothes, waved them above his head. He circled around him, scrutinizing him from all angles.

"Take off your shoes," he said. Jimmy nudged the heels down and kicked them off. Everett snatched them up and turned them over and over in his hands.

Jimmy looked at Everett and grinned. "Was it real or was it an illusion?"

"Sweet Jesus," Everett said.

Jimmy looked at Everett, his eyes serious. "You're right about one thing. The time is close. It isn't Apocalypse, Rev. Gamble, it's Ascension. People's souls don't need to be saved; they need to be healed. They're not going to be raptured; they're going to be transformed right here on this earth. If they're ready. And most aren't. We have to get them ready."

"Ready for what?" Everett asked. "Who's we? You talking about you and me?"

"Ready to save themselves and this planet," Jimmy said. "And, no, I'm talking about Susan and me."

Everett's jaw dropped open. "You and that little old girl."

Will couldn't believe his ears.

"Susan's the first," Jimmy said. "The call has gone out. Others will come. The world is full of souls that need healing."

"Lordy, son," Everett said, "that's the last thing the world wants."

"We'll see," Jimmy said.

Everett snorted. "Fool's errand, if you ask me."

Jimmy smiled. "Do you remember the story about giving a starving man a fish or teaching him how to fish?"

Everett cut his eyes at Jimmy. "I know you're fixing to deprive me of my livelihood."

"I don't want you to suffer," Jimmy said, "or any of the folks that come here." He nodded at Will. "Mr. Diamond promised to take my place."

Will was thunderstruck. "What are you talking about?"

"Your dream," Jimmy said. "You do remember your dream?"

"How do you know about that? I never told anyone, not even Susan."

"You made a promise, Mr. Diamond."

"I didn't," Will said. His chest felt painfully tight, his heart hammering on it like a drum.

"You asked what you could do," Jimmy said, looking steadily at Will. "You said there must be some way God could use you. You said you'd do anything."

Will had started feeling nauseous when Jimmy asked him about the dream. "I don't remember," he said. Or was it that he didn't want to remember. Now with Jimmy pressing him, the dream came rushing back: the old man that never stopped changing, the thing made of light and sound that talked inside Will's head, being trapped in the column of light and the darkness reaching for him, hungering for him. 'Your blood will be the cure.' That's what the thing had said. And Will had agreed to it. "I'll do it for Susan." He had heard himself say it. That's what had freaked him out. Why he'd woken up in a panic. He had been standing there – wherever there was – watching himself. And Susan had been there, though he didn't know how that was possible. And Jimmy Gamble, he had been there, too. That's why he looked familiar when Will saw his picture in the paper. But a dream wasn't real. It couldn't be real.

"The dream was real, Mr. Diamond." Jimmy said, as if reading Will's mind.

Will didn't care anymore what was real and what wasn't. He didn't care if Jimmy Gamble could heal the sick or if he had really risen up into the sky without wires. What difference did it make if Susan had gotten wise blood from some loser disciple? He didn't care if Jimmy Gamble was Jesus on a stick. He didn't care and he didn't have to do anything he didn't want to do.

"Susan's cured, right?" Will asked.

Jimmy studied him for a long, uncomfortable moment that caused Will to drop his gaze and stare at his shoes.

"Of course," Jimmy said, "nothing can change that." A look of disappointment flickered across his face. But it was gone in a second and he smiled and offered Will his hand.

"Good luck to you then," he said.

Relief flooded through Will. The world was getting back to normal. He reached for Jimmy's hand. He saw the boy's lips moving and strained to hear, but couldn't make out the words. As the tips of his fingers grazed Jimmy's hand, every muscle in Will's body locked; he was paralyzed. The surface of his skin began to tingle, then burn, until he felt as if he was being pricked by hundreds of needles. Will stared dumbly at the blood flowing from his palms, vaguely registered the slippery sensation in his shoes, and the viscous wetness soaking through his shirt. He watched, in shock, as the speed of the flow increased and blood gushed from him like a ruptured water balloon. Will stared in disbelief at the spreading pool at his feet. There was so much of it he wondered if it was all the blood he had in his body. A sliver of hysteria shot through him. His now rubbery legs collapsed and he grabbed for Jimmy to keep himself from going down. As he stumbled forward he saw blood pooling in Jimmy's palms. Blood that rose up and leapt at him like an animal as Jimmy gripped his hands and hauled him up.

A scream dissolved in Will's throat as liquid light surged through him. The pain in his ankle and his head were gone. And he knew if he looked at his side, where the car had hit him, the bruise would be gone. The scars on his wrist, from his hand crashing through a plate glass window, had disappeared. In a moment of manic silliness he wondered if his hair had grown back. Then the elation passed, and he was left with a feeling of such calm and utter completeness it left him on the verge of tears. Still holding onto Jimmy's hands, Will gazed into his eyes dreamy and uncomprehending,

"Not everyone can endure wise blood," Jimmy said, "but Susan can. And believe it or not, Mr. Diamond, so can you."

Susan ran to Jimmy's side. She wrapped her arms around him and hugged him. Earl Dean followed her. Everett sidled up next to Will and looked him over. "You sure he can take your place? You fix him up did you?" he asked looking sideways at Jimmy.

Earl Dean shook his head and laughed out loud. He clapped Will on the back. "Lord," he said, "I reckon any fool's a tool."

"Now, Earl Dean, don't be unkind," Jimmy said. "We should thank Mr. Diamond for the sacrifice he's made. He was reluctant. But you can't blame him. Now he's healed of everything that ever ailed him, and he can heal others by the power of his blood."

"Well now," Everett said, "I don't know how I'm going to explain it." He was eyeing Will's hands and side, and the rosy blotches blooming through his tennis shoes. "Sure isn't much to look at, but I reckon he'll do."

"He'll do just fine," Jimmy said.

There was golden light in the new blood spreading through Will's body, and nothing, anywhere in his whole entire being hurt. His heart thumped softly in his chest, and at its center was a swirl of something that sounded like voices and felt like music, a wonderful something that became a tiny, bright kernel of secret knowledge that made him gasp.

Printed in the United States
201446BV00037B/1-18/A